"AND THEY'RE OFF!"

Prancer burst out of the gate, immediately taking the lead. But that wasn't what was supposed to happen. Stephen, the jockey, was supposed to hold her back until the last part of the race, when he'd been told to make her go as fast as she could. Carole watched Prancer carefully, and the look of the horse told her that nothing was going to stop her. The horse who loved to run fast by herself, alone on the practice track, wanted the utter joy of running by herself, ahead of the rest of the field on the racetrack. Prancer's legs flew back and forth so fast Carole couldn't even see them land. Stephen had sensed the urgency in the horse's gait and had given her all the rein she needed to run wild and free, ahead of everybody else.

Even from across the track, Carole was sure she could hear the pounding of Prancer's hoofbeats, so rapid as to be a single throbbing sound.

And then something happened. . . .

THE SADDLE CLUB

RACEHORSE

BONNIE BRYANT

A BANTAM SKYLARK BOOK®
NEW YORK · TORONTO · LONDON · SYDNEY · AUCKLAND

I would like to express my special thanks to Dorothy Campbell for her inspiring tale and to Caroline Ring and the Tamarack Pony Club for their inspiring enthusiasm.

—B.B.H.

RL 5, 009–0012

RACEHORSE

A Bantam Skylark Book / April 1992

Skylark Books is a registered trademark of Bantam Books, a division of Bantam Doubleday Dell Publishing Group, Inc. Registered in U.S. Patent and Trademark Office and elsewhere.

"The Saddle Club" is a trademark of Bonnie Bryant Hiller. The Saddle Club design/logo, which consists of an inverted U-shaped design, a riding crop, and a riding hat is a trademark of Bantam Books.

ISBN 0-553-15983-6

Published simultaneously in the United States and Canada

Bantam Books are published by Bantam Books, a division of Bantam Doubleday Dell Publishing Group, Inc. Its trademark, consisting of the words "Bantam Books" and the portrayal of a rooster, is Registered in U.S. Patent and Trademark Office and in other countries. Marca Registrada. Bantam Books, 666 Fifth Avenue, New York, New York 10103.

PRINTED IN THE UNITED STATES OF AMERICA

CWO   0 9 8 7 6 5 4 3 2 1

For D.M.G.

Racehorse

"HORSE WISE, COME to order!" Max Regnery called.

Carole Hanson thought those were some of the sweetest words in the English language. It meant that her Pony Club meeting was about to start. Her Pony Club was called Horse Wise. Usually, the best Pony Club meetings took place on horseback. This one was going to be an exception, though, because they had a special speaker. Judy Barker, the stable's vet, was going to be talking to the group today. Anything Judy ever had to say about horses was interesting to Carole.

Carole settled down cross-legged on the floor between her two best friends, Lisa Atwood and Stevie Hanson. The girls exchanged excited glances. This was going to be fun, but that wasn't news. Pony Club meetings were always fun—especially when you were completely surrounded by friends!

Carole loved horses and anything to do with horses. She'd been riding since she was a little girl and expected to keep on riding for the rest of her life. She had her own horse named Starlight and she tried to ride him every day.

Carole boarded Starlight at Pine Hollow, the stable owned by Max Regnery. Her two best friends, Lisa and Stevie, were very different from Carole, but all three of them had one big thing in common: horses. They all rode horseback at Pine Hollow and they all loved horses so much that they'd formed their own club. It was called The Saddle Club and it only had two requirements. The first was that members had to be horse crazy. That was easy. Horses were just about the only thing the girls ever wanted to talk about. The second requirement was that members had to be willing to help one another out whenever they needed it, no matter what the problem.

Thinking about that reminded Carole of some of the problems the girls had solved in the past. That made her smile.

Lisa and Stevie were both members of Horse Wise, too, and they were right next to Carole at the meeting. Lisa, the oldest of the threesome, looked like the youngest. She was small and slender, with a creamy complexion, wavy light brown hair, and freckles. Lisa was serious and methodical about everything she did, including horseback riding, which she'd only started doing about a year ago. She was a straight-A student at school and always tried to do everything people expected of her. That wasn't easy when all her parents wanted was for her to be perfect! Still, Lisa seemed to manage it, most of the time, and the best part, as far as her friends were concerned, was that she managed it without being a goody-goody.

Stevie was very different from Lisa. She had long dark blond hair and hazel eyes that sparkled with mischief because that's what was usually on her mind. She scraped by in school, spending an undue amount of time in the office of the dean and/or the headmistress of the private school she attended. However, events had shown that Stevie usually had a way of coming out on top, no matter how deep the hot water.

Carole, with wavy black hair, dark brown eyes, and dark skin, had an intense look about her, when the subject was horses. When the subject was anything else, Carole could be something of a flake. It amazed her friends to recall the time when they went on an overnight trail ride with Carole. She had forgotten her own backpack and sleeping bag, but remembered to bring every possible combination of backup equipment for the horses. Carole was definitely tuned into horses and now she was very eager to listen to Judy Barker.

"A healthy horse is essential to good riding," Judy began. "And the most important health care a horse gets is from its rider."

Carole hadn't ever thought of it that way, but, of course, it made sense. It was the rider's responsibility to know the horse well enough to recognize when something was wrong. That was the time to get off the horse, check it carefully and, if necessary, call the vet. There were always riders who thought they could get away without calling the vet—that the problems would just go away, but horse health problems rarely just "went away." Without care, they only got worse. Carole knew that. So did just about every other Horse Wise member at the meeting.

The group, which included fifteen members at this meeting, followed Judy and Max to the paddock next to the stable at Pine Hollow. Like Max, Judy believed that the best way to learn was to do. She told the pony clubbers they should each go get the horse they usually rode and secure their lead ropes around the edge of the paddock so they could all work together at the same time. She also told them to bring their grooming buckets.

Carole found Starlight in his stall, contentedly munching on some hay. She clipped his lead rope to his halter and brought him to the paddock, picking up her grooming bucket along the way. Stevie brought Topside, a Thoroughbred horse that had belonged to a championship rider, Dorothy DeSoto, until Dorothy had an accident that would keep her out of competition for the rest of her life. Max had been only too willing to provide a home for the wonderful gelding, and Stevie was thrilled to be able to ride him.

Lisa rode Pepper, a dappled gray gelding who had been a member of the stable for many years. Pepper was a great horse for all riders, but particularly for beginners. He had a way of instructing even the greenest greenhorn, and Lisa had been very glad for that quality in him more than once. She gave him a big hug as she brought him out to his spot at the edge of the fence, between Stevie and Carole's horses.

All of the riders had learned how to groom their horses, and the girls began the job as Judy spoke. She explained that grooming was an excellent time to check the horse's physical condition.

"Remember, your hands must always do two jobs as you work on grooming your horse. The first is simply grooming. The second is to check for soundness as you go."

"What's this?" Meg Durham asked, pointing to a small raised lump, about a half an inch across, on Patch's leg. Judy went to examine.

"Anybody know?" she asked. Lisa raised her hand. Judy nodded.

"Patch is allergic to flies," Lisa said. "I bet it's a fly bite."

"I bet you're right," Judy said. "The lump will go away

on its own in a short while. In the meantime, the best thing you can do for Patch is to spray him for flies. Where do we keep the fly spray?"

"On the medicine shelf in the tack room," Meg said automatically. Then, without further instruction, she went indoors to retrieve it.

As she worked on Starlight's coat, Carole thought about Pony Club meetings. It seemed that every question a member asked was answered with another question. The pony clubbers were supposed to have all the answers—and a lot of the time they did.

Lisa worked hard on Pepper. She loved his gray coat, and she loved to make it shine by cleaning it. In return, he usually seemed to love being cleaned. She wasn't sure if it was the fact that he loved the feel of the brushes, cloths, and combs, or if it was because he knew how nice he'd look when it was done. She actually suspected it was because he enjoyed being the center of somebody else's attention. Today, however, he was acting very uninterested in the whole process.

She automatically checked his vital signs as she worked, noting that his breathing rate was normal and his pulse was normal. These were all good news. She was concerned, however, and her face must have shown the worry, because Stevie quickly noticed it.

"What's wrong?" Stevie asked. "Is Pepper sick?"

Lisa shrugged. "He just doesn't seem very interested in

6

the grooming. It's like he's not alert or something. Is that sick?"

"Not really," Stevie said. "It's the way I usually am in school. Sick isn't the word my teachers use to describe me." She could make a joke out of anything. Lisa wasn't sure this was something to joke about.

"Look," Stevie went on. "It's probably just that he doesn't feel in top condition because he's not well groomed yet. Wait to see how he feels when his coat's shiny, okay?"

That made sense to Lisa. She redoubled her efforts to make him clean, but when Judy came to check on her progress, Lisa asked her about his apparent listlessness.

Judy checked him quickly to be sure nothing was going wrong. Then she smiled reassuringly. "He's just getting old." She carefully opened Pepper's mouth and showed Lisa the horse's teeth. "Look at the wear on these teeth and the angle of Pepper's jaw. Max probably knows for sure, but I would guess Pepper is somewhere in his mid-twenties. In horse equivalent years, that makes him nearly ninety. Don't worry if he seems a little un-enthusiastic sometimes."

Ninety?! That certainly explained it. "I guess I have to be really careful with him, don't I?" Lisa asked.

"You have to be really careful with all horses," Judy reminded her. "And Pepper's advanced years just go to show you what good care will do."

Lisa returned to the job of grooming Pepper. At ninety he definitely deserved the best she could give him.

Carole was ready to clean Starlight's hooves. As she'd learned to do, she began with his right front hoof and ran her hand straight down his leg to the hoof. Doing this accomplished three things: It let Starlight know where her hand was, which was important, because horses could get nervous if they didn't know what was happening; it allowed her to check his leg as she went; and finally, it was a way of telling him what was coming.

This time, however, her hand didn't make it all the way to the hoof. She stopped short at the knee. She felt something odd. She lifted her hand, put it above the knee again, and ran it downward again. She still felt something odd. There was some swelling at Starlight's knee.

"Judy," she called out. "Something's wrong with Starlight."

Judy came right over.

"Look, when I run my hand down his leg, it feels warm and swollen at the knee."

"Just the right knee?" Judy asked.

Carole had been so concerned that she'd forgotten to check his left leg. Whenever something didn't seem right, the first thing to do on a horse was to check the opposite side for comparison. Carole was embarrassed to have forgotten to do that, but she also knew what she would find. Starlight was her horse and she knew his legs very well. His left leg wouldn't have the swelling she'd detected in his right leg. It would feel normal. She checked and she was right.

"Yes," she said. "It's just the right one."

Judy felt for herself. She asked Carole if she'd noticed that Starlight was limping or favoring the leg. She hadn't. Carole unclipped the lead rope and led him around the paddock while Judy observed carefully.

"Well, that's the good news," Judy said. "Whatever it is, it barely shows in his walk yet. That means that we've caught it early before much damage has been done."

Carole knew what she meant. About the worst thing a rider could do with a horse was to work him when he was lame. That could make a small injury turn into a permanent problem.

Judy checked the knee several more times carefully and made her pronouncement to the whole group, who had been watching.

"It could be a couple of things," she said. "But they all come down to the same prescription for now. Does anybody know what that prescription is?"

"Complete rest," said Betsy Cavanaugh.

Judy nodded.

"Bandages," Polly Giacomin suggested.

Judy agreed.

"Hose the joint," Carole said. "That's almost like a

massage, and it reduces inflammation, which helps healing."

"Very good," Judy said.

Carole was pleased that everyone knew how to care for the horse, but the problem was "complete rest" meant that Carole wasn't going to be able to ride Starlight until the leg was healed. They'd been riding together almost every single day since Christmas, when her father had given him to her. She couldn't imagine a day without a ride on Starlight.

"How long will Starlight need rest?" she asked.

Judy shrugged. "It's hard to say, Carole. If it's a mild carpitis and the swelling comes down quickly, then maybe as little as two weeks. If it isn't, and it doesn't, we might need to take an X ray, and then we'll just see. It's hard to tell. All I can say for sure is that he needs rest, bandages, and hosing twice a day for twenty minutes."

"Oh, Carole, that's terrible," Stevie said. "Poor Starlight!"

"And poor you," Lisa added. Both of her friends knew how hard it was going to be for Carole not to be able to ride Starlight for two weeks. And what if it went on for longer than that? Carole shook her head, trying to shake off the thought.

"It's okay," she said bravely to her friends. "The important thing is that it's probably not very serious and Starlight will recover. All I have to do is to take care of him."

She smiled, trying to reassure all the Horse Wise members who were feeling sad for her.

Carole clipped Starlight's lead rope back to the eye hook on the paddock fence. A thousand questions were rushing through her head. How could this have happened? What could she have done to keep it from happening? Would Starlight heal quickly? Would he heal at all? Was he in pain? What should she do first?

The first thing she wanted to do was to hug her horse and apologize for whatever had happened. She also wanted to bury her face in his soft mane and cry. She wanted to cry for him because of his injury. She also wanted to cry for herself because she wouldn't be able to ride for so long. Two weeks. And what if it had to be longer than that?

Carole didn't want to think about that. She'd certainly cry then, and that wasn't a good idea in front of everybody else. Instead of crying, she got to work. She patted Starlight affectionately and went into the stable to fetch some bandages. That, at least, had the advantage of getting her away for a few minutes so if she did cry, nobody would see.

The stable was nearly empty because most of the horses were in the paddock. Mrs. Reg, Max Regnery's mother and the stable's manager, was at her desk off the tack room, busily scribbling something. It took Carole just a few minutes to locate the leg bandages and to choose one for Starlight. She started back toward the paddock.

"Oh, Carole!" It was Max. He was coming out of his own office and he was beaming. Something had made him very happy. Carole was glad someone was happy. "Have I got good news!"

"I need it," she said.

"What's the matter?" Max asked, concerned that his star pupil was so upset. It wasn't like Carole to be unhappy at Pine Hollow. Carole explained about Starlight's injury.

"It happens, Carole," he said matter-of-factly. "Horses get injuries. One of the reasons I make my riders all learn to be caretakers is to minimize injuries, but the fact is that they happen, and it's a part of horseback riding. You and Starlight will learn from this."

Knowing Max was right didn't make Carole feel better. It just made her feel more petulant.

"This isn't what I want to learn right now!" she complained. "If I can't ride for two weeks, there's nothing to look forward to!"

"Oh, yes, there is," Max said. Then his smile returned. "Definitely, there is. Come on, I've got some news for everybody."

Carole was doubtful, but Max was her instructor and her friend. She held the leg wrap tightly in her hand and followed him.

"Don't stop working," Max instructed the pony club-bers. "Just work and listen at the same time, because I've got some news."

Fifteen Pony Club members picked up combs and brushes and pretended to work while Max talked.

"I've just been speaking with a former student of mine. It seems that she's been spending some time working with a student of hers who is going to be appearing at a horse show in the western part of the state two weeks from today. She suggested that she come over here the follow-ing day and have a reunion of sorts—"

"Dorothy DeSoto?" Stevie blurted out. "She wants to see Topside!"

"—with the horse she rode in the ring for so many years," Max continued.

"Oh, it's going to be great to see her!" Stevie said.

Max gave Stevie a dirty look. "Do I get to finish, or do you know the rest of the good news?"

"There's more?" she said. Max nodded. "Then it has to be that she wants to actually ride Topside!"

"Who's doing the announcing? You or me?" Max asked.

Stevie thought—or at least *hoped*—that he was sort of laughing. She blushed and promised herself to keep her mouth closed until Max was done.

"Ahem," Max went on. "Miss Dorothy DeSoto will be here on Sunday, two weeks and one day from today. She will be reunited with her championship Thoroughbred, Topside, and she will perform a dressage demonstration for anybody and everybody who wishes to watch. I will be sending invitations to all of my students, present and former, to come see it. This will, of course, include any interested Horse Wise members. Are there any interested Horse Wise members?"

Fifteen hands shot up. Dorothy DeSoto was the best. There was no way anybody who cared about horseback riding would miss this chance.

Carole understood then what Max had meant about something to look forward to over the next two weeks. Since Dorothy's performance was scheduled for that day, two weeks and one day after today, it might be the first day she would be able to ride Starlight. It would, indeed, be a wonderful day. Excited by the thought, she decided to give Stevie an extra hand.

Stevie gave Topside a final coat of hoof polish while Carole held his lead. He seemed to understand that something special was coming, and Stevie wanted to be sure he would look his absolute best for Dorothy. Of course, he'd have to be groomed several times between now and then, and he'd get an even more special grooming before the performance, but still, Stevie found the whole idea inspirational, and Topside appreciated the attention. His ears perked up. His tail swished regally. He was getting ready, too. The girls were pleased with the results.

Nearby, Lisa picked up a few strands of Pepper's tail and began brushing them carefully. Tails worked best if you only brushed a few strands at a time. It took longer, but now that Lisa knew Pepper was in his nineties, she was determined to make him look better than ever.

THE SADDLE CLUB, new though it was, had already established a few traditions. One of them was that, whenever possible, they had Saddle Club meetings at TD's after Horse Wise. TD's was an ice cream parlor at the local shopping center. TD stood for Tastee Delight, but the place was universally known as TD's.

The girls slipped into their favorite booth at their favorite hangout and settled down to talk about their favorite subject: horses.

"I can't believe Starlight is lame," Carole said.

"He isn't really lame," Stevie said, trying to console her. "He's just got a sore knee. You have to take care of him now so he won't *get* lame."

"I know, I know. Judy isn't worried and I guess I

shouldn't be, either, but the fact is that I can't ride him for at least two weeks. What am I going to do?"

"Well, you're going to spend a lot of time taking care of him for one thing," Lisa said reasonably. She was the best of the three at being reasonable. Sometimes her friends wished she weren't *so* reasonable, but in the long run, they were usually grateful for it.

"Of course, you're right," Carole agreed, reasonably. "In fact, I'm going to have to run cool water on his knee twice a day for twenty minutes. That'll keep me busy for forty minutes every day. What am I going to do with the other twenty-three hours and twenty minutes if I still can't ride? I know Max would let me ride Barq or even Delilah, but the fact is that he has to charge me if I ride a stable horse, and taking care of Starlight is taking up all of the Hanson family budget on horseback riding. What am I going to do?"

Nobody had to answer that question for a minute because the waitress came to take their order. The waitress made a very impolite face when she saw Stevie. Stevie was famous for odd combinations of ice cream and toppings. They were also often very complicated. This time, however, her order was simple.

"Pistachio ice cream with caramel topping," she said.

The waitress smiled wanly and wrote down the order. Lisa ordered a dish of vanilla frozen yogurt. Carole just wanted some chocolate ice cream.

Stevie turned back to Carole. "You can help Max organize everything for Dorothy DeSoto's visit. Isn't it great she's coming?" Stevie asked.

"She's about the best there is in dressage," Lisa agreed, "and that's really good for you."

Stevie nodded proudly. Dressage was one of the most precise types of riding there was, and it amused both Lisa and Carole that their friend, Stevie, a very imprecise person in most ways, was the best of the three of them at dressage. Somehow, all the joking, all the wildness, all the vague schemes, disappeared from Stevie the minute she was working on her dressage. Max had bought Topside from Dorothy because she'd never be able to ride him in competition again, but he had also bought him so that Stevie would have a really good horse to work with. The Saddle Club suspected he hoped for great things from Stevie someday.

"What were you and Judy discussing about Pepper?" Carole asked. She'd been concerned about Starlight, but not so concerned that she hadn't noticed Lisa working extra hard on the old gray horse.

"I was just worried that he seemed sort of off his feed. Judy explained that it's just old age. I figured out that he's almost twice as old as I am in human years, and in horse years he's older than my grandmother. Actually, he's about as old as my great-grandmother would be if she were still alive—and if she were, I don't think she'd be carrying riders around on her back. Pepper is really some-thing!"

"Maybe he's getting too old to be ridden," Carole said. "It happens, you know."

"I know," Lisa said. "Max and I were talking. He said I should ride Comanche and get used to him because Pep-per is coming pretty close to retirement."

"Hard to picture Pepper in a rocking chair," Stevie mused, leaning back so the waitress could give her her sundae. All three girls heard the woman grunt dis-pleasure looking at the green-and-beige concoction. Ste-vie smiled beatifically.

The girls dived into their treats as soon as the waitress had gone. There was little talk for a few minutes.

When they heard a familiar voice at the take-out counter, they all looked up. There was Judy Barker, or-dering a pint of ice cream to take home.

"Hi, girls!" she greeted them and then she joined them. "Great meeting today, wasn't it?" she asked.

"It was if you don't mind news like the horse you love is getting too old to ride," Lisa said a little more sharply than she had meant to.

"Or if you like the idea of not being able to ride at all for two weeks," added Carole. "What am I going to do? And even if we can figure out what I'll do for two weeks, how on earth am I going to survive if Starlight isn't better by then?"

"I'm sorry, girls," Judy said. "I was so excited about Dorothy's visit—remember we were in our beginner riding classes together at Pine Hollow more than twenty years ago—that I wasn't thinking about your troubles. Anyway, your problems aren't so impossible."

"Easy for you to say," Carole retorted. Then, realizing how sharp it had sounded, she immediately apologized.

"That's okay," Judy said. "I do understand. And I also have a suggestion. For you, Lisa, it's easy. Max wants you to ride Comanche, and I think you two will get along well. Comanche is more spirited than Pepper, but you're ready for a more spirited horse. I think you'll like him." She turned to Carole. "For you, it's a little different. I could say things like you just have to get used to the fact that horses have medical problems and that's a fact of life."

"Oh," Lisa said. Everybody looked at her.

"What's the matter?" Stevie asked.

"The word 'life,'" she answered. "It just reminded me that I have a paper to write for school. The subject is 'Life.'"

"Yuck," Stevie said, and Carole rolled her eyes. But the two of them were more interested in talking about Starlight than Lisa's paper, so they continued the conversation with Judy.

"I know what you're saying is true," Carole said. "It's

just that I don't like it. I'd rather ride and tend to a healthy horse than not be able to ride a sick one."

"Working with sick horses is what I do for a living," Judy reminded her. "You always seem to enjoy working with me."

"Oh, I do, but you know what I mean. . . ." Carole let the thought drift.

"I know what you mean," Judy said. "And I have a suggestion. Since you can't ride and you will be tending to one sick horse, why don't you spend your after-school hours over the next two weeks tending to a lot of sick horses? Why don't you work with me?"

"Could I?" Carole asked eagerly.

"As long as your father agrees," Judy told her. "I suspect he will, too, because I talked to him about it on the phone about a half an hour ago, and when I suggested that we might swap your assistance for my care for Starlight, he seemed to like the idea a lot. He said something about getting a moping girl out of his hair. . . ."

Carole smiled for the first time since she'd found the swelling in Starlight's knee. That was a real solution. It would give her something concrete to do, and it would also give her a way to allay one of the unspoken problems about Starlight's knee, and that was the expense of veterinary care. Judy was more than fair with her bills, and her dad would never complain, but the fact was injuries were expensive. Carole was only too happy to be able to help with that. She put out her hand to shake. Judy took it.

"Deal," she said.

"Look, I'll check Starlight every day around three-fifteen—that's when you get there after school, right?"

Carole nodded.

"Then we'll leave from there. I promised your father I'd have you home in time for dinner."

"Terrific! Now all I have to do is convince Dad to serve dinner at ten-thirty!"

Judy laughed at Carole's joke as she stood up from the table and promised to see her on Monday.

"Well, that takes care of *your* problem," Lisa said. "Now what about mine?"

"Pepper?" Stevie asked. "I thought the solution is that you're going to ride Comanche."

"Not that one," Lisa said. "Comanche's a nice horse. I'll get used to him eventually. No, I mean the problem about my paper. Don't you think the teacher's assigned a rather large topic? *Life?*"

"It's one of those topics where it's sometimes harder to figure out what you're going to leave out than what you're going to include, isn't it?" Carole observed.

Lisa realized, with a little prick of her conscience, that she might have hit a nerve in Carole. Carole's mother had died a few years ago, and it was obviously still very vivid. Life and death were issues that Carole had a great deal of reason to understand better than her friends did. Lisa was sorry she'd raised the subject.

"I don't think it's all that complicated," Stevie said, keeping the topic open. "I think that some of the things that have happened today are issues of life and death. After all, look at how Pepper is getting older, closer to his own death. We've been thinking of it from your point of view, but of course, there's his point of view, too. Wouldn't that make a nice topic for the paper?"

Lisa smiled and nodded. "Yes, it would," she said. "I think you're really on to something and that makes this a red-letter day."

"How's that?" Stevie asked.

"I think it's the first time—and probably the *last*, too—that you've ever actually helped *me* with my homework. Thanks."

She gave Stevie a hug, and then they all set about finishing their ice cream.

3

JUDY BARKER'S PICKUP truck bounced along a dirt road that snaked uphill toward a horse farm.

Carole, sitting in the passenger seat, gripped the armrest on the door to keep from bouncing right out of her seat. "Why on earth is this place so hard to reach?" she asked. Her voice sounded funny to her because she was being jostled so much.

Judy smiled. "This is nothing," she said. "In fact, this place is easy to reach, compared to some of my clients' places. One of the facts about the life of an equine vet is that we do make house calls—no matter where the house is—and in this case, it's on the top of a mountain!"

Carole looked out the window and across the Virginia hills at the scenery. The land swept downward, the rich green of the fields in constant motion. A neat white fence enclosed each of the fields, stretched along the contours of the hillside. It was Carole's favorite kind of view. Knowing that it was all for the benefit of the horses, she didn't mind the bouncing so much.

"Who's our patient here?" she asked.

"It's a mare, about to foal," Judy explained. "She's had trouble before. She even lost her last foal, but this time everything's going smoothly. I don't even really need to be here, but the owner wants to be sure we don't slip. He loves this mare a lot. He was upset about losing the foal, but he was even more worried that something might happen to the mare. He's a very cautious man. That's the kind of owner I like best."

Carole agreed with that completely. Working with Judy had taught her that too many owners waited too long to call the vet. Small problems became big ones when they weren't attended to in a timely manner.

This was the third day Carole and Judy had been working together. She was having so much fun and learning so much that it almost made up for not being able to ride Starlight. Each day after school, she headed for Pine Hollow, removed Starlight's bandages and ran water on his leg to stimulate the healing, and then rebandaged it. Carole felt that Starlight missed their daily rides as much as she did, but he also seemed to like the attention he was getting. From a medical point of view, the good news was that the swelling wasn't getting any worse. Judy felt it would still be a while before they would see any improvement. So far, she was pleased with what *wasn't* happening.

The truck took a final bounce and then the road turned up to the left. There were the barns and stable. Judy drew her traveling hospital to a halt, checked her book, handed the mare's file to Carole, and the two of them stepped out of the truck.

As soon as Carole saw the mare, she knew why the owner cared so much about her. She was a chestnut with a pretty face and a sweet disposition. Fortunately she also had a healthy pregnancy going on, and it took Judy only a few minutes to assure the owner there were no problems developing. Judy told the owner that she would be back in a month, and within a matter of minutes they were again bouncing on the dirt road—this time downhill.

"One of my favorite kind of vet calls," Judy remarked. "I *love* to visit a healthy horse."

"Particularly one as sweet as that," Carole echoed. "So what's next?"

"A horse of a different color," Judy said.

That turned out to be an understatement. Their next call was at a breeding stable nearby. The stable's stallion seemed to be having a problem, and the owner wanted Judy to check him out.

Carole didn't get to see too much of stallions. Most male riding horses were gelded, which made them unable to breed but gave them better dispositions and made them calmer and more reliable. Stallions tended to be high-spirited, temperamental, and unpredictable. The stallion they were visiting was all of those things, and then some, because he wasn't feeling well.

Judy checked him over, being careful of the horse as well as herself. She had him cross-tied at the back of his stall and never let herself get blocked from the doorway. A high-spirited horse, especially one who wasn't feeling well, could be very dangerous.

Judy wouldn't let Carole into the stall, but she did let her hold the needle and the vials she used to draw blood. Carole wasn't sorry to be kept out of the stall. Normally she wasn't at all afraid of any horse, but in this case she made an exception. It made her think about the fact that a vet was often at risk when working with a horse like that stallion. She was still thinking about it when Judy's visit was all done and they were on their way to the next call.

"Aren't you afraid sometimes?" Carole asked as they drove away.

"All the time," Judy said. "I wouldn't still be on my feet if I weren't. The minute I stop being afraid—well, maybe 'alert to danger' is a better term than 'afraid,'—is the minute I'll be in real trouble. Horses are big animals. They are bigger than I am, that's for sure. I have to respect that. Of course, the thing I never do is let the horse know I'm afraid. That's even more trouble than not being afraid. You know how competitive horses are. They are always trying to get the upper hand."

Carole knew that was true. Horses seemed to have a way of sensing people's fear and taking advantage of it. Their natural competitiveness made them constantly sensitive to vulnerability in others, even people. It was a quality Carole loved and admired in horses. She also respected it.

"Speaking of horses that are competitive, our next stop is going to be a change of pace for you. Most of my clients have regular riding horses, jumpers, show horses, and hunters. This one is different. He's got racehorses."

"Thoroughbreds?" Carole asked.

"Very," Judy said.

Horse breeds were interesting to Carole. Each different breed was known for different characteristics. Arabians, for instance, were known for their beauty and endurance. Quarter horses were famous for their bursts of speed in short sprints. The "quarter" in their name referred to quarter miles, which was about as long as they could race flat out. Standardbreds trotted fast; Morgans were both strong and fast. Draught horses, like the famous Clydesdales, were incredibly big and strong. No breed, however, was better known, or more admired, than Thoroughbreds. These were the horses of racetracks. Many horses used for routine riding, jumping, showing, and hunting, were also Thoroughbreds, or had Thoroughbred blood in their family trees, but the best and the fastest of them were the most valuable and went to the racetracks to run for money.

"Is one of them sick?" Carole asked.

"No," Judy said. "We're visiting healthy horses again. It's just that the owner is racing a couple of his horses soon and wants me to check them out and make recommendations on how to have them in top form for their races."

Carole hunted through the stack of files Judy carried with her at all times and brought out the ones marked "Maskee Farms," for their next visit. She found they were checking on a four-year-old stallion named Hold Fast and a three-year-old filly named Prancer. Looking through the files, she could see that everything was thoroughly documented as was the case with all of the horses Judy took care of. She could also see that these horses had more care and attention than most of Judy's patients. The owner didn't let anything slip his attention. It made Carole feel that he loved his horses as much as she thought all owners should love theirs. She liked the man—David McLeod—even before she met him.

Maskee Farms looked pretty much like every other well-run stable she'd ever seen—only more so. Everything was spotlessly clean and in perfect repair. Carole couldn't find a cobweb, even when she put her mind to it. Mr. McLeod came out to greet them at the truck. He nodded politely when Judy introduced him to Carole, but his whole focus was on his horses. He was talking about them and about the races they were going to be in before Judy had a chance to open her door.

As he led the way into the stable, he talked about things Carole was only vaguely familiar with. Not surprisingly, he was concerned about how the horses would run and where they would place in their races. What did surprise her, though, was his expectation.

"The stallion is in a field of eight, and I'd like to see him in the top five," Mr. McLeod said. "The jockey thinks he can do better, but I don't want to push him."

Carole had expected him to think his horses would win every race.

Judy looked at the chart quickly and then examined the horse.

"I don't think you have to worry about pushing him, Mr. McLeod," she said. "I'll do a blood count, but I think he's in top form."

"You think I'll be able to sell him for a good price then?"

Sell? That surprised Carole, too. She expected that people who owned horses did it because they loved them. How could he be thinking of selling the horse?

"Definitely," Judy said. "This horse will do well as long as he's healthy, and he is that," she assured Mr. McLeod.

Once again they looked at the charts, carefully planning the program for Hold Fast. As they talked, Carole looked around the stable.

Every one of the horses there was more beautiful and better taken care of than any horses Carole had ever seen before. Each one was groomed to a silky shine. Fresh, sweet-smelling straw covered the floors, and the place was brightly lit. Carole thought that was less for the horses' benefit than it was for the owner. Good lights allowed an owner to see problems easily. Everything here, it seemed, was set up for the horses' safety and benefit, and everything that contributed to the horses' safety and benefit would help the owner when the horses were on the track. And, she realized, the only reason they were on the track was to make money for the owner.

Carole had been riding and loving horses for a long time. Now that she owned Starlight, she'd become even more aware of the fact that it could be very expensive to own a horse, but mostly all she cared about was being able to own and ride him. Today, for the first time, she was seeing something else about horses: They were a business. Mr. McLeod appeared to love his horses every bit as much as Carole loved Starlight, but he also expected to profit from caring for them. That was a totally new idea to Carole. It made her see Maskee Farms in a new light. It made her think of horses in a new way.

She scratched her head and looked around once more.

There was a gentle sound behind her. She spun around and found herself face-to-face with a sleek and beautiful bay, who was leaning curiously out of the stall. The bay sniffed at Carole and managed to tickle her on her neck. Carole giggled. The horse sniffed some more. Carole did the only logical thing. She hugged the horse, who seemed to respond warmly. Then Carole stepped back. It felt undignified to be hugging a Thoroughbred racehorse, probably worth hundreds of thousands of dollars. Still the horse was a horse, and horses, as far as Carole was concerned, were lovable.

"What's your magic?" Mr. McLeod asked, surprising Carole. Judy was with him.

"Magic?" Carole echoed.

"Your magic with Prancer, I mean. I've never seen her be affectionate before. She gave you a first class smooch!"

Carole blushed. "I guess she did. She's just so gentle—"

"Yes, and maybe too gentle," he said, sighing. "She's got more gentle in her than she has speed."

"You mean to tell me that this sweet horse is a racehorse?" Carole was surprised.

"That remains to be seen," Mr. McLeod said, shrugging. "She's three years old and hasn't raced much before this. Her bloodlines are impeccable, but there's something missing. . . ."

Carole looked at the mare. She had four legs, a tail, a

mane, a head, and everything else Carole thought essential to a horse. "What's missing?" she asked.

"She's got the sweetest disposition of any horse I've ever owned," Mr. McLeod said.

"But what's missing?" Carole persisted.

"That's it," he said. Then he smiled, understanding Carole's confusion. "You know the story about Ferdinand the bull? He was a total failure in the bullring because he just wanted to smell the flowers?"

Carole nodded. She knew the story.

"Well, I don't think Prancer has the drive to compete. She's fast enough. She certainly does respectable times on the practice track, but when she's competing with other horses, it's like she doesn't want to hurt their feelings and win. But maybe she has a few surprises for me. Although she's always been gentle and easy to handle, she's never been as affectionate with anybody as she was with you just then. Maybe that's what's been missing."

"What?" Carole asked.

"True love," Mr. McLeod said.

Carole thought he was joking, but when she looked at him, she could tell he wasn't.

"If a horse really cares about something—or someone—it can help that horse do things that are otherwise impossible. So far, Prancer hasn't seemed to care very much about winning. I'm giving her a chance to prove me wrong at the next meet. I've got a lot of money tied up in Prancer. She's going to have to come through for me, or I can't afford to feed her anymore."

There it was again—money. Carole had to do some more thinking about that aspect of horses. She stepped back and let Judy examine Prancer and go over the medication records. Although she wanted to listen, she found that Judy and Mr. McLeod seemed to be talking a new language, and it all became a blur. The only thing that remained clear to her was that Prancer was as pretty and sweet a horse as she'd ever known, and it was very hard to understand why Mr. McLeod was so obviously disappointed in her.

4

LISA GLANCED AT the clock over Ms. Ingleby's head. There were twenty minutes left of English, and then she could go. She usually loved school, especially Ms. Ingleby's class. Today, however, she was meeting Stevie at Pine Hollow and they were going for a ride. If it came to a choice between English and riding, well, riding would always win. The minute hand on the clock jumped forward. Nineteen minutes.

There was something else bothering Lisa, though. She was a little nervous about the essay on "Life" that she had handed in on Monday morning.

When she came into class today, she'd spotted the stack of papers on Ms. Ingleby's desk. The teacher had definitely finished grading the essays and would be returning them soon. Lisa sighed. She dreaded seeing her grade.

The problem was, Lisa was used to getting A's. It was just about the only grade she ever got, and she didn't like getting anything *but* an A. In her essay she'd written about Pepper and the fact that he was getting old, but she'd also written some things about his life. She knew that her essay was very sentimental, and she wasn't at all sure that essays should be sentimental. Yet somehow she hadn't been able to help herself. She felt sentimental about Pepper.

Ms. Ingleby cleared her throat. That was a sign that the moment was coming. Lisa shifted uneasily in her seat.

"Now, about these papers," Ms. Ingleby began. She had a few general comments to make. They had too many spelling mistakes and grammatical errors. Most of the students also needed to work on their handwriting. She had noticed quite a few of them had awfully wide margins—"As if I can't tell that that was simply designed to make a two-page essay fill three pages," the teacher added dryly. There were titters in the classroom.

"A few of you don't seem to understand what an essay is, and I've made notes on your papers that you should see me after class. . . ."

Lisa could already imagine the tracks of red ink on her paper and the demands that she come to special-help sessions.

"Many of you who have done well on most of the work this year just had trouble with this assignment. . . ."

Ms. Ingleby would probably be sending a special note home to her parents about Lisa's dropping grade.

"And some of you will have to revise your papers." There were groans around the classroom. Lisa's mind raced. She was trying to figure out when she'd have time to do it all over again—and what she'd do.

"But one paper was especially interesting," Ms. Ingleby said. "It won't surprise any of you to find out who wrote it, and I think a lot of you will know exactly what the student was talking about, so, without ado, I'm going to read it to you."

Ms. Ingleby picked up a paper from the top of the stack and began reading. At first Lisa didn't recognize her own words. Then, when it sank in that Ms. Ingleby was reading *her* essay, she blushed deeply, aware that her classmates were already looking at her. They knew who had written it.

Her essay began with general statements about life— that it was a gift whose value could only be measured by the good that the life contributed to the world. Then she got down to the business of Pepper.

Pepper is Pine Hollow's gentlest, sweetest, kindest horse. He's every first rider's first choice. He is so attentive to his rider's needs that he makes riding seem easy. In fact, one time I was riding Pepper, unaware that we were in a field that housed a fierce bull. We were too far from the gate to get to safety, so Pepper did the only logical thing—he taught me to jump in one easy lesson! We both landed safely on the other side of the fence. I think I can say truly that I owe Pepper my life.

Now his life is coming to an end. His gray coat, once dark and dappled, is now white and dappled. His head, once held high with pride, often seems too heavy for his neck to hold up. His eyes, once sparkling and alert, are now rheumy and clouded with cataracts. His ears splay awkwardly, dulled to the familiar sounds around him. He is old.

I love him as he is, for that is how I have known him, but I like to think of him as he was.

Pepper was a champion, not because he got ribbons, though he surely did, but because he taught me and many other riders how to love horses—starting with him. And we do.

There was a long silence in the classroom when Ms. Ingleby finished reading the essay. Lisa looked straight ahead, embarrassed. She wasn't usually embarrassed when a teacher read her work, but in this case, she didn't think she'd done a very good job. She didn't feel as if she'd written about life as much as she'd written about Pepper. Nobody else seemed to have noticed, however.

Lisa was jolted out of her embarrassment by a gentle sniff from the girl named Eleanora Griffin sitting next to her. Eleanora was crying.

"You mean I can't ride Pepper anymore?" she asked.

"Not much more, I guess," Lisa said. "Maybe Max will be using him for walks with really little kids. But he won't be doing regular classes again."

"Oh, wow, I remember Pepper," a boy two rows back said. "I rode him the only time I ever rode a horse!"

Then the class seemed to erupt with memories of Pepper. It turned out that more than half the class had, at one time or another, been to Pine Hollow and remembered Pepper, either because they had actually ridden him—or because they wished they had.

"I remember Pepper, too," Ms. Ingleby said, breaking up the pandemonium. "I rode Pepper when *I* was a little girl. He was a lot younger then. Lisa wasn't kidding when she said he'd been around a long time!" The students laughed.

The rest of the class was spent with various students talking about their memories of Pepper. Lisa had been worried that her essay was too sentimental and too personal. She'd also been worried that it hadn't been right.

Something seemed to her to be missing about it. Nobody else seemed to feel that way and everybody agreed with her feelings about Pepper. That comforted her a little bit and by the time the bell rang, Lisa was almost sorry class was over. Almost, but not really, because then it was time to go to Pine Hollow and be with Pepper. She wanted to see Pepper, but she also wanted to shake her own feelings of doubt about the work she'd done for the essay. She practically ran to Pine Hollow.

"COME ON, LISA," Stevie said, welcoming her to the stable. "I've cleared it with Max for us to take a practice ride in the outdoor ring—me on Topside, you on Comanche. You're going to love him."

One of the things Lisa loved about her friend was that Stevie understood exactly how she was feeling about Pepper and was trying to help her think positively. Of course, one of the reasons Stevie understood was that she felt the same way about Pepper that everybody else did. Pepper had been one of Stevie's first horses as well. Stevie, however, wasn't one to dwell on sad thoughts. Her mind always headed straight for the fun side of things. To Stevie, it was exciting that Lisa was going to get a chance to learn more about a whole new horse. Except, of course, Stevie had ridden Comanche before.

"I'm not so sure about this," Lisa said uneasily.

"Comanche's great," Stevie assured her.

"Great for you," Lisa said. "I'm not so sure about me."

Early on in her riding, Lisa had learned that horses, like people, had very individual personalities, and for a rider to enjoy a horse meant that their personalities had to mesh. One of the reasons she'd gotten along so well with Pepper was that he was sweet and even-tempered. Comanche, on the other hand, was high-spirited and mischievous. That made him a perfect match for Stevie, not necessarily for Lisa.

"Come on, chin up," Stevie said. "Let this young boy show you his stuff, okay?"

"Okay," Lisa agreed, though she wasn't honestly enthusiastic about the change. They headed for Comanche's stall. On the way they passed Pepper. He looked up when Lisa passed and sighed heavily. It was as if the thought of going out on a ride was too much for him. Lisa thought he seemed relieved when she walked on by, though how could he really understand?

Stevie had gotten to Pine Hollow first and had tacked up Comanche for Lisa. She'd also groomed him quickly so that his deep chestnut coat was gleaming and he stood proudly, anticipating a fun time with his rider. His eyes sparkled and his ears perked alertly. He nodded a greeting to the girls, apparently eager to be riding. The contrast between Comanche and Pepper was startling. It was certainly enough to convince Lisa that this was worth trying.

The two girls brought their horses into the outdoor ring, touching the traditional good-luck horseshoe on their way through the doorway. Lisa always did that automatically, because by tradition all the riders at Pine Hollow did it. Nobody who had ever done it had gotten seriously hurt riding at the stable. Today she wondered if it would be enough. After all, Comanche was a lot more horse for her to control than Pepper had been. She was going to have to work harder. She was going to have to be better.

Red O'Malley, the head stablehand at Pine Hollow, was nearby to keep an eye on the girls. He waved jauntily at Lisa. He was always nice, but he didn't usually do that. Lisa realized that he understood what was going on. He wanted Lisa to like Comanche, too.

Lisa and Stevie circled the ring a few times at a walk, allowing the horses to warm up. The warm-up also permitted Lisa to get used to the feel of Comanche's gait. Horses' gaits were as distinct as their personalities. Lisa thought that Comanche couldn't have been more different from Pepper. For one thing, he was a full hand taller. Horses were measured by "hands," and a hand was four inches. That meant Comanche's saddle was four inches higher than Pepper's. Lisa noticed the difference right away. It was like sitting in the cab of a truck instead of the front seat of a car. The world looked smaller. Comanche's walk was also brisker than Pepper's. Since his legs were longer, each stride carried him across more ground. Also, there was a sort of grinding quality to Pepper's slow walk. Lisa knew that had to do with his age. Comanche seemed to take pride in the smoothness of his walk.

Then they trotted. Comanche's trot was almost choppy, but it was very fast. Lisa could feel the breeze in her hair, even with her hard hat on. She posted automatically, rising and sitting ever so slightly with every step of the horse's trot. Pepper's trot was very smooth, though much slower than Comanche's. She often did a sitting trot on Pepper. It would be hard and uncomfortable to sit Comanche's trot. She was sure she'd just bounce out of the saddle like a cumbersome sack of potatoes. Lisa wasn't happy about that at all, and she told Stevie about it.

"Balance," Stevie said, consoling her. "Balance is the most important thing. When you work on that, you'll find you won't have much trouble with that choppy trot."

Lisa made a face.

"I promise," Stevie insisted. "And besides, the best is yet to come."

Stevie slid her foot back and touched her horse, Topside, behind his girth. In an instant he began cantering.

Comanche followed suit. It bothered Lisa that Comanche had started cantering before she'd signaled him to do it. It just wasn't a good idea to let a horse change gaits on his own, even if she was about to tell him to do it. Lisa tugged on the reins ever so slightly. Immediately Comanche slowed to a trot. That was good. She made him trot a quarter of the way around the ring. Then she gave him the signal for a canter. He obeyed. At first Lisa was so pleased by the fact that she'd done the right thing and taken charge of Comanche that she didn't even notice how wonderful the result was. Then it came to her. Comanche had a smooth, rocking canter that totally made up for his choppy trot. She sat deeply in the saddle, shifting easily back and forth with the gentle motion of the speeding horse.

"Oh, this is wonderful!" she called out to Stevie, now behind her.

"I knew you'd love him!" Stevie said happily.

But, of course, that wasn't what Lisa had said. She *didn't* love Comanche. She just loved his canter. The horse she loved was Pepper, and the trouble was that she couldn't ride him. Riding wasn't ever going to be the same for Lisa.

5

ALTHOUGH CAROLE LOVED being with Judy and learning from her, she found it difficult to be with horses who were in pain. They had been working together for a while and Carole couldn't get over her feelings of sadness every time she saw a sick horse.

"It's not the pain they're in that's important—unless it was avoidable," Judy said to her. "It's how we can get them out of it that matters."

The two of them sat across from one another at a pizza restaurant where they'd paused for a snack in the middle of a busy afternoon.

"But it hurts me so much to see a horse who feels bad," Carole explained.

"All creatures, including people, feel bad from time to

time. Most of what we see is temporary and will pass. You know the gelding we saw earlier with founder?"

"I thought you said that was laminitis—"

"Same thing, different name," Judy told her. "It's an inflammation in the hoof. I recommended a change of diet, a new kind of shoe. Within a short time that horse will be back under saddle. For that horse it's a temporary condition. For another it's chronic and will recur dozens of times throughout his life. I don't feel sorry for the gelding we just treated. I do feel sorry for the horse with a chronic problem. Life can be tough."

"I know," Carole said. "I guess I just don't like to be reminded of that."

"I'm sorry," Judy said quickly, giving Carole a comforting look. Before she could say more, her beeper went off. She hurriedly took a final bite of the pizza, grabbed her soda, and dashed for her truck, parked outside the restaurant. "Let's see what Alan wants."

Alan was Judy's husband and veterinary assistant. He didn't usually call her unless there was an emergency. When veterinary emergencies happened, seconds counted. Judy was on her car phone calling Alan before Carole had a chance to climb into the cab of the truck.

"Hold on!" Judy said, hanging up the phone and turning on the engine at practically the same instant.

Carole slammed her door and strapped herself in with

her seat belt. When they'd made a U-turn and were speeding along the street, Carole asked what was up.

"I won't know for sure until I see, but it sounds to me like we've got a really sick horse on our hands. This one may bother you, Carole. You don't have to come in, you know."

"What happened?"

"I think it's tetanus," Judy said, shifting into high gear.

Tetanus? Carole knew all about tetanus. It was everywhere. It was caused by a bacteria that lived in the soil and horses were constantly exposed to it. It was a tough germ that could survive for long periods and in extreme temperatures. Everybody who knew anything about horses knew a lot about tetanus—including the fact that it was almost completely preventable. Every horse had to be immunized against it soon after birth, with regular boosters throughout their lifetimes. Every person who spent time around horses had to be immunized against it regularly. Any cut, particularly deep ones, on people and horses, had to be assumed to have tetanus in it and called for additional immunization. Tetanus was a dreadful disease. It was also a killer.

Judy drew the truck to an abrupt halt at a small barn on a small farm and jumped out of the cab almost as fast as she'd gotten in.

The horse's owner, looking drawn and pale, was waiting for Judy by the entrance. He came over while Judy took her bag out of the traveling emergency room on the back of the truck, and the two of them talked urgently.

Carole reached for the handle of the door and then stopped. She didn't know if she could do this—if she was ready to see a horse who was deathly ill. She'd seen death in humans and horses before, and she didn't like it. She looked at the hand reaching for the door handle. It was shaking. Then she thought about the horse inside the barn who needed Judy's help and might need hers as well. She decided that her own feelings were not as important as the horse's care.

Without further hesitation, Carole opened the door and joined Judy and the owner in the barn.

Carole saw the sick horse immediately. He was standing in a soiled stall, all of his limbs stiff from pain. His head was raised in an awkward position, almost like an extension of his neck. His eyes looked clouded until Carole realized that it was the horse's "third" eyelid—a milky membrane that was always open—that had closed over them, as if trying to shut out the world. Saliva drooled freely from his clenched jaw. Then Carole saw the healing gash on the horse's hind leg that was the cause of the disease. The gash was getting better. The horse was not.

Judy didn't waste any time. She began examining the horse and jotting notes in a file.

Carole knew some of the things Judy would do. She also knew that if this horse was going to have a chance, he was going to need a clean stall, specially prepared for him. Immediately she began working on that. One of the stalls in the barn was empty. She mucked it out, removing every bit of soil and old straw. She covered the bottom of the stall with a thick layer of fresh sweet straw. A horse who couldn't bend his neck was going to need his water bucket up high. She found a high nail and hung a fresh water bucket from it. She removed the low hooks and nails because they might cause further damage to a stiff and flailing horse.

As soon as she was done, Judy walked the stiff gelding over to the clean stall, smiling a small thank you to Carole for knowing what to do and for doing it without being told. Carole would have been glad for some help from the owner, but he looked as shaken as his horse and seemed totally incapable of doing anything useful.

Judy gave the horse an injection, gave the owner some instructions, and left the horse in peace. It was all they could do for him right then. It would probably be all they could ever do for him.

When the three of them stepped outside the barn, Judy turned to the owner and said what was really on her mind. She told him that he was almost certainly going to lose the horse—over eighty percent of horses with tetanus don't make it, and virtually all of the small percentage who do make it receive treatment long before the disease has reached this stage.

"Now, let me see the immunization records for your other horses," Judy said.

The man looked at her blankly.

"When did the others receive their last tetanus boosters?" she demanded. Her voice sounded harder and harsher than Carole had ever heard it. Carole realized that Judy was very angry and was trying, unsuccessfully, to mask it.

"I don't have any records," the man said. "My horses haven't been sick before."

Judy took a deep breath. "You have six horses in that stable," she said. "I am going to immunize each one of them against tetanus today. Today you are going to start taking proper care of your horses or I will never come here again."

The man nodded meekly. Judy returned to the barn to immunize the other horses. Carole returned to the truck. She was close to tears and couldn't shake the horrible image of the sick gelding in agonized pain. She couldn't face the reality of it for one more minute.

When Judy and Carole left, they rode together in silence. There was nothing to say. The image of the horse with tetanus was with them both and said it all for them.

"IT MUST HAVE been awful," Stevie said later, trying to comfort Carole. Carole, Lisa, and Stevie had met up at

TD's for a fast visit after Judy's vet calls. They were having an impromptu Saddle Club meeting until Carole's father picked her up on his way home from work.

"I've never seen a horse in such pain," Carole told her friends.

"I hope I never do," Lisa said. She swished her spoon idly around in her root beer float. Carole's story about the gelding with tetanus had taken her appetite away. "You know, all people who own horses should be required to belong to Pony Clubs and pass the Pony Club tests. Max would never let any of his students do such stupid things."

"That's what I told Judy," Carole said. "She told me it was too bad that horses don't come with instruction booklets."

Stevie put her arm around Carole's shoulder. "If it's so hard to be with sick horses, maybe you shouldn't go out with Judy again," she suggested.

"That was hard. Definitely," Carole said. "But there are other things that aren't hard—that are really wonderful. I wouldn't want to miss a minute of those. As a matter of fact, I've even got some good and exciting things to tell you about."

"Like what?" Stevie asked.

"Well, for starters, right after we saw the horse with tetanus, we visited a newborn foal. He was born last night. He looked like he was all legs with a little bobtail that he flicked. He cuddled up to his mother and I watched him nursing. I could practically see his little tummy filling up with milk, and then he lay down to take a nap. He sort of sighed happily before he fell asleep. He was about the cutest thing I ever saw."

"Did that make up for the sick horse?" Lisa asked.

"Not exactly," Carole said. "But what happened at the next place we stopped certainly did."

"Yes?" Lisa asked. She took a sip of her float and waited expectantly.

"Well, remember the guy with the racehorses—Mr. McLeod?"

"Yes?" Stevie replied.

"We went back to his stable for another check on the horses who are going to race. You wouldn't believe how much care those horses get. It was a great antidote to the stable with the sick horse, I'll tell you. Anyway, I got to see Prancer again. She's this sweet mare. . . ."

Carole enjoyed talking about Prancer, and her friends loved hearing every detail.

"So when is Prancer going to race?" Stevie asked.

"A week from Saturday," Carole told her.

"Too bad you can't be there to watch," Lisa said.

"But that's the good news," Carole said, her eyes lighting up mischievously.

Two pairs of eyebrows shot up.

"You can?" Stevie asked. "Is your father going to take you?"

"Nope, Judy is. See, Mr. McLeod wants Judy to be there and she invited me. It's pretty common for owners to bring their own vets. I'm just lucky enough to be this vet's assistant. Can you believe it?"

"Of course I believe it," Stevie said logically. "It makes complete sense to me. And I bet Prancer will run better because of you."

"I don't know about that," Carole replied, "but I do know I'll have fun and learn an awful lot. Can you imagine what it will be like to be at a racetrack, the place absolutely filled with incredibly valuable horses?"

Lisa pushed away the root beer float in front of her, staring at the milky residue left on the glass. "Horses are funny," she observed.

"Well, Prancer definitely is," Carole began. "You should have seen the way she nuzzled my neck—"

"No, that's not quite what I meant," Lisa interrupted. "I mean, you know I wrote that essay about Pepper for school, just the way Stevie suggested. The teacher really liked it because she thought it meant something to so many of the kids in the class, though I didn't think it was very good. But it isn't just Pepper who means a lot and who can show us things. Look at the day you just had. You saw death, you saw birth, you saw health and sickness. You saw just about everything, all within a couple of hours. What an afternoon!"

"Yeah," Stevie echoed.

"Definitely," Carole agreed, once again flooded by mixed feelings of joy and sadness.

6

LISA WAS STILL thinking about The Saddle Club meeting at TD's when she arrived at Pine Hollow the following afternoon. She and Stevie had agreed to take care of Starlight for Carole for one day so that Carole and Judy could get an earlier start. Lisa and Stevie were more than willing to take care of Starlight. He was a wonderful horse, and he didn't really need much care.

Lisa paused at Pepper's stall and gave the horse a good hug, which he seemed to like. She also gave him the carrot she'd brought from home. He crunched down on it and chewed contentedly. Lisa gave him another hug and moved on to Starlight's stall.

Stevie had beaten her to the job. She'd removed Starlight's bandages and was leading him over to the hosing area.

"I think the swelling is beginning to go down," Stevie said, pointing to Starlight's knee.

Lisa approached the horse cautiously and then ran her hand down along his leg until she got to the joint. She could feel the swelling all right. She was pretty sure it wasn't any worse. She just wasn't sure it was better.

"I don't know," she said.

"Me neither," Stevie conceded. "I guess I'm just hoping."

"I'm sure he's going to be all right. After all, he's getting the best care in the world, isn't he?"

"Not compared to what Carole was telling us about those racehorses. Boy, wouldn't you like to be able to see that? And isn't Carole lucky to be going to the racetrack?"

"She sure is," Lisa said. She reached for the hose while Stevie cross-tied Starlight. "I'd give just about anything to be there with her."

"So would I." Stevie turned the spigot and the water came gushing out. Lisa squeezed the hose, forcing the water into a strong stream, and aimed it at Starlight's swollen knee. They had to do it for a few minutes, but it was all they had to do. It wasn't hard work, and Starlight apparently enjoyed it. At least he stood still for it, and that allowed Stevie and Lisa to talk.

"Have you ever been to a racetrack?" Lisa asked.

"No, but my parents go sometimes," she said. "As a matter of fact, they were talking about going again soon."

"How soon?" Lisa asked.

Stevie looked at her and her face lit up. "What a great idea!" she said. "I'll start nagging them about it right after dinner!"

"Do you think it'll work?" Lisa asked.

"It will if I have anything to say about it," Stevie assured her. "And I can tell that I already have a lot to say about it. I know they're not going anywhere this weekend. My mother has been talking about building a rock garden near the swimming pool. Every time she talks about it, my dad gets this look of desperation. I have the funny feeling he'll be only too willing to go to the racetrack. But will your parents let you go?"

"You know my parents, Stevie. They think your parents are wonderful—and of course, they're right. So if your parents say it's okay, they'll let me go."

Stevie turned off the water and began toweling Starlight's leg gently, massaging the swelling as she did. When Starlight was completely dry, the girls took him back to his stall. Stevie watched while Lisa put a fresh wrap on his knee.

"You've learned a lot in a little while," Stevie said.

"My friends are good teachers," Lisa told her.

"I guess so. And you must be, too. Isn't it funny that just last week *I* was giving you help on a school assignment, and now today *you* were coming up with a scheme that will get us to the racetrack? The whole world is turning upside down!"

Lisa laughed. It was nice to think that the best parts of Stevie were rubbing off on her!

"How's it coming, girls?" Max asked, peering over the door to Starlight's stall.

"Just fine," Stevie told him. "We think the swelling is going down. Maybe. A little bit."

"Glad you're so certain," he said, chuckling. "But don't worry. As long as it's not getting worse now, it's a good sign. When you're waiting for a horse to heal, patience is a good quality."

"At least *he's* healing," Lisa said. Max looked at her in surprise. She had even surprised herself by how harsh the words sounded coming from her own mouth. One of the things she really liked about Max, though, was that you never had to spend a lot of time explaining the obvious things.

"How did it go with Comanche?" he asked.

Lisa shrugged. "Okay, I guess."

Max scratched his chin. "You know, I just stopped by and checked on Pepper. He seemed a little restless to me. I think he could use some gentle exercise. Would you have time to take him out on a trail ride—say a half hour—if somebody could go with you?"

"Like me? On Topside?" Stevie asked.

"Like you, on Topside," Max confirmed.

"I bet we could squeeze it in," Stevie said, keeping a straight face.

"Don't get Pepper overtired," Max said. "Mostly just walk, a little trotting, and no cantering."

"We can definitely squeeze it in," Lisa said.

"Thanks," Max said. "I'd do it myself, but . . ."

He didn't finish the sentence. He didn't have to, because nobody was fooling anybody and everybody knew it.

Lisa checked the work she'd done on Starlight's leg. Stevie double-checked it and they were both satisfied. They stood up. There was a sparkle in Stevie's eye.

"Race you to the tack room!" Stevie challenged.

"Last one in the saddle is a rotten egg!" Stevie countered.

They were off.

Ten minutes later Topside and Pepper were ready for their trail ride. So were their riders, still breathless from the race to mount up. Stevie had won the race, but that was because Pepper was just slower than Topside when it came to walking to the mounting area. It didn't matter at all. What mattered was that they were ready to go.

The girls each touched the good-luck horseshoe. Red O'Malley, amused by their excitement, opened the gate for them, and they were off—at a walk.

"I really love this horse," Lisa said. "He's just so gentle." Pepper nodded his head as if he agreed.

It was a fresh day in the late spring. All around the girls, wildflowers were in bloom, and new grass shoots filled the rolling fields. The trees in the woods were feathered with diminutive leaves, bursting from the buds on each branch and twig. Lisa might not have noticed these things except for the fact that they seemed to be at odds with the sweet, gentle, aging horse beneath her. If that was the case, though, Pepper was oblivious to it. He continued walking, surely and steadily, wherever Lisa told him to go.

"Want to trot?" Stevie asked.

"Of course," Lisa said.

Topside and Pepper began trotting at the same time. Although Topside was in the lead, Pepper took the change of gait as a challenge. He picked up his head and lengthened his stride, speeding faster and gaining on Topside. It never failed to surprise Lisa to see how naturally competitive horses were—even old horses, near retirement.

"Just goes to show that you can't keep a good horse down!" she said brightly, speeding past Stevie. Topside was not going to be outdone. He instantly picked up his own pace and the two horses crossed the field side by side, trotting happily.

As the girls neared the woods, they drew in on their reins and brought the horses back to a walk.

"That was wonderful," Lisa said.

"And I think Pepper enjoyed it as much as you did," Stevie said.

"More," Lisa said. "And, you know, it turns out that

Pepper has been enjoying this kind of thing with a lot of people for a long time."

"How's that?" Stevie asked.

"Remember the essay I wrote? It was sort of surprising about Pepper."

"What was surprising? You didn't get an A?"

"Yes, I got an A, although I don't really think I deserved it, but that wasn't the thing I wanted to tell you about. It was the thing about Ms. Ingleby reading it out loud in class."

"I had a teacher do that once," Stevie said. "She wanted to make a point about my writing. See, I'd broken some kind of school record by using the word 'but' five times in one paragraph. I wanted to die."

"That wasn't why Ms. Ingleby read my paper," Lisa went on. "But I would have wanted to die, too, if it had been. But I probably would have survived. But my parents would have heard about it, and they would have killed me, but they might not have. They—"

"Enough. I get the point," Stevie said, giggling. "So why did Ms. Ingleby read your essay?"

"Because she liked Pepper. It turned out that practically every kid in my class had ridden Pepper at one time or another. A lot of them were pretty upset that Pepper is getting old. One girl, Eleanora Griffin, was even crying."

"I remember Eleanora. She used to ride in our class. Then her mother got this idea that horseback riding was dangerous, and she had to give it up. She really adored Pepper."

"She still does," Lisa assured her. "And you know what? Even Ms. Ingleby had ridden Pepper when she was a little girl. *That's* why she read my essay. It was kind of neat. It's like this one horse ties a whole lot of people together. Isn't that odd? I mean, how many riders have sat in this saddle, on this horse, and enjoyed it as much as I'm enjoying it now?"

"Hundreds, I guess," Stevie said. "It makes it seem all the more as if Pepper had earned his retirement, doesn't it?"

"Yes. Too bad we can't give him a black-tie dinner and a gold watch to take to Florida. I think he'd be happier with some warm mash anyway. What is the matter with you?" Lisa had just noticed an odd look cross Stevie's face.

"Me? Nothing's wrong," Stevie said. "Nothing at all. Let's trot again, okay?"

Both Pepper and Topside heard the word before the riders gave them the signals. They began trotting easily and smoothly. Lisa was so pleased by the refreshing ride that she forgot until much later to try to pump Stevie for an explanation about the funny face she'd made. When she recalled it again, Lisa dismissed the idea. After all, Stevie was as famous for making odd faces as she was for thinking up wild and wacky ideas. It was probably really nothing at all.

7

For Carole the next few days seemed to fly by. She couldn't learn not to hurt when she and Judy were working with a horse in discomfort or pain, but she did learn to accept that it was a vet's job to heal horses, especially when they were really sick. She cried when she learned that the gelding with tetanus had died.

"Did you know he was going to die?" Carole asked Judy as they drove from one call to another.

"I never *know*," Judy said. "If there's one thing I've learned in all the years I've spent doing this, it's that horses surprise me—even more than people. I find it helps to hope for good surprises and not to expect the bad ones, though they will, of course, come."

A long silence filled the cab of the truck. Carole truly understood what Judy was saying.

"Today, if possible, I just want us to have good surprises," Judy said.

"If it's all good, will that be a surprise?" Carole asked, teasing.

"Indeed it will," Judy told her. She turned the truck into a circular drive then and pulled to a halt in front of a small barn where there was a small pony with a small problem. The two of them examined the pony named Luna because of the perfect half-moon on his face. Carole and Judy were very aware of the fact that the pony's young owner, a little girl named May, was watching everything they did with a hawk's eye.

"You're not going to hurt my pony, are you?" May asked. She patted Luna's neck vigorously and protectively as she talked to Judy.

"I promise," Judy said. "You called me because you noticed your pony wasn't feeling well. That was the right thing to do. I checked him last week and found that he has some worms in him. I'm just going to give him some medicine to kill the worms. He may not like the medicine an awful lot, but he certainly is going to like feeling better. You were right to call in the first place."

Carole knew that worms were something that horses just got. They were around barnyards, paddocks, and fields. Almost every horse had problems with parasites at one time or another, and as long as the vet came promptly and treated the horse, the worms wouldn't be any real problem, just a short-term nuisance. Untreated, worms and other parasites could cause devastating damage to a horse. May had been right to have her parents call Judy at the first sign of trouble.

While Judy dosed the pony, Carole talked to May about the Pony Club at Pine Hollow. The little girl was so eager to learn how to take care of her pony that Carole was sure she'd want to participate in Horse Wise. By the time the pony had been treated, May was ready to sign up. Carole promised her she'd be welcome at the next meeting on Tuesday.

"Nice job," Judy said as she and Carole pulled out of the driveway. "You kept that little girl so busy talking about Horse Wise that she never had a chance to flinch while I put the tube down her pony's throat to deliver the medicine to his stomach. What a team we make!"

"I guess," Carole said. "And to tell you the truth, I got so busy telling her all about Horse Wise that *I* never noticed what you were doing—even when I was holding the horse's head for you!"

Judy laughed and so did Carole. They both liked the fact that they'd left a healthier horse and a more knowledgeable owner behind.

"Next stop, Maskee Farms."

"Again?" Carole asked. She certainly wanted to return, but she was surprised that it was necessary.

"Again. It's for a final check on the two racers for this coming weekend."

Maskee Farms was just a few miles down the road, and Mr. McLeod was waiting for them. He waved a cheerful greeting and then met them in the stable.

"How are my patients doing?" Judy asked.

"Just fine, I think, though I'd like you to take a close look at Prancer in action. I think she might be favoring one of her hind legs a little."

"All right," Judy said. "Let's see her moving."

Mr. McLeod gave Carole a lead rope and nodded, indicating that Carole should bring Prancer out. Prancer's eyes seemed to sparkle when she saw Carole, and Carole felt just the same way. She clipped the rope onto the horse and brought her out of the stall, leading her to a ring off the rear of the stable.

At Judy's instruction, Carole led Prancer in a walk and then a trot, running in front of her, though it was hard to keep up with the Thoroughbred racehorse's trot. She *was* fast!

"Looks okay to me," Judy said.

"Maybe," Mr. McLeod said. "But you should see her at a faster gait."

"Why don't we saddle her up?" Judy suggested.

"I don't have anyone to ride her," he said. "She's not used to the weight of somebody like me or you. . . ." His eyes landed on Carole, still holding the horse's lead. "What about her?" he asked.

Carole could hardly believe what she was hearing. Mr. McLeod was actually suggesting that she have a chance to ride a valuable horse like Prancer? She quickly decided that she'd heard wrong. He probably just wanted her to lead the horse some more and run faster.

"Great idea," Judy said. "Carole's a terrific rider. Where's the saddle?"

She had heard it right. He actually wanted her to ride Prancer! She was so excited, she barely noticed what she was doing as she tacked up the mare.

Racing saddles were much smaller than regular English riding saddles. The less weight a horse had to carry, the faster it would be able to run. That was the main reason why most jockeys were so small and so thin. Still, a saddle was a saddle, and a horse was a horse. Carole had no trouble tacking up Prancer and only a little trouble adjusting to the very short stirrups that were also part of a racing saddle. What it meant, mainly, was that she had to have a boost from Mr. McLeod to get into the saddle. And then she was there, on the back of a beautiful, sweet racehorse. It seemed like a dream come true.

Judy and Mr. McLeod waited for her to accustom herself to the feel of Prancer. That didn't take long. Prancer's motions were smooth, almost seamless. Her training had been for speed. Every movement she made was sleek. Carole thought it was almost as wonderful as riding Starlight.

First Carole walked Prancer and then brought her to a trot. She felt very self-conscious as Judy and Mr. McLeod watched every single thing she did, but then she realized they weren't watching her. They were watching the horse.

"Want to try a round on the practice track?" Mr. McLeod asked.

"Me?" Carole said, realizing immediately how dumb that sounded.

"Yes, please," he said, ignoring her silly question. He opened the gate to the ring and showed her the way to walk Prancer to his practice track.

"You don't want to go full out," he said. "Because we don't want to tire Prancer. Judy and I just want to have a chance to observe her at her faster gaits. Take her two-thirds of the way around the track at a trot. Pick up a canter at the far turn and bring her back in front of us at whatever speed she's comfortable with. Don't push her. She likes to go fast. Your main job will be to hold on."

It was a main job Carole was more than willing to take on. She looked at Judy for reassurance. Judy nodded proudly, grinning. Carole began the circuit of the racetrack that Mr. McLeod had practically in his backyard.

It was easy. Prancer had obviously done this many times before, and she knew just what to do. Carole barely had to give her any instructions at all. They walked a few steps and then began an easy trot. Carole gave the horse a little leg as they proceeded, picking up the pace of the trot. She wanted to be at a fast, working trot by the time she was ready to change gaits.

Carole had spent many happy hours on horseback, but she'd never had the feeling she had now. There, stretched out in front of her, was a racetrack—almost a mile long, marked off at eighth-mile lengths. She and Prancer were the only ones on it. She felt as if they were the only ones in the world and certainly the only ones who mattered. There was nothing to distract the relationship between her and the horse. Everything rested between them.

Prancer's pace quickened without any signal from Carole. It was what Mr. McLeod had meant when he'd promised her that the horse had speed. Just at the moment they made the far turn, Carole moved her outside leg back behind the horse's girth and she instantly changed to a canter. Carole put a little more pressure on Prancer with her legs, and the mare's canter quickly lengthened and changed to a gallop. Automatically Carole rose in the saddle, leaning forward to maintain her balance over the horse's new center of balance at the new gait. She could feel Prancer's mouth on the bit, ready to respond in an instant to a new command from Carole. She could also feel an incredible surge of power pounding beneath her. Prancer was doing everything Carole could want her to do. She let the horse have all the rein she needed. Prancer took it and flew with it.

It was an exhilarating feeling beyond anything Carole had ever known on a horse. It wasn't just a matter of speed, either. This was the very thing this horse had been designed and trained to do for every minute from the moment of her birth. She performed perfectly, joyously, the dirt track flying beneath her feet, and Carole enjoyed each second. The white fence bordering the track seemed to stream into a single line, and the eighth-mile poles seemed to come together, brought closer by the horse's speed. Nothing mattered at that moment except what felt like the near perfect union of horse and rider—and speed.

Then she realized that she had passed Mr. McLeod and Judy, flying by with Prancer's glorious gallop. She tugged gently on the reins and sat down in the saddle. As fast as the horse had started, she slowed, first to a canter, then to a trot. Finally she walked. She wasn't even breathing hard, though Carole was.

She could still feel the glorious motion of the ride on Prancer, long after it had stopped.

She walked the horse back to Judy and Mr. McLeod. "Nothing wrong with this horse," Judy pronounced.

"Nothing wrong with the rider, either," Mr. McLeod said. "Nice job, Carole. Did you have fun? Uh, don't bother to answer that. I can tell by the grin on your face. She's quite a horse, isn't she?"

Carole sighed with pleasure. "Yes, she is," she said, when she could talk.

"Well, you rode her well, and she seems to like you a lot. I was about to invite you to come to the track this weekend, but Judy tells me you're already planning to be there."

"You *want* me there?" Carole asked. Once again, Mr. McLeod was surprising her. She couldn't believe what she was hearing.

"I sure do, and my jockey will be glad you're there, too. He'll be pleased to know that somebody Prancer likes so much will be around. She'll race better."

"She will?"

"Oh, I don't know for certain," Mr. McLeod said. "I just know that a happy horse is usually a fast horse. This horse is happy with you."

"And I'm happy around her," Carole replied.

"I CAN'T EVEN tell you what it was like," Carole whispered to Lisa the following Tuesday at their Horse Wise meeting. Stevie craned her neck to listen, too. "I think we were going a thousand miles an hour—"

"I don't think racehorses go more than about fifty," Lisa said sensibly.

"You know what I mean," Carole said.

"No, perhaps you'll tell us," Max said pointedly. They were having an unmounted meeting and were sitting in Max's office at Pine Hollow supposedly talking about horse parasites. All Carole wanted to talk about, however, was the incredible ride she'd had on Prancer and how she was actually going to be at the racetrack to watch the filly run. However, she didn't want to talk about those things in the middle of a Pony Club meeting.

"Sorry, Max," she said sheepishly, noticing that everybody, including Horse Wise's newest member, May, was staring at her. Carole blushed.

Max cleared his throat authoritatively and resumed the meeting. "Now, who can tell me about parasite control in stable horses?" Max asked. May's hand shot up.

Racehorses were out; parasites were in—at least until The Saddle Club had a chance to get to TD's after the meeting.

The minute Horse Wise was finished, the three girls made a dash for TD's, slid into booths at the ice cream shop, and ordered their treats. Then Carole told her friends absolutely everything about riding Prancer and how wonderful it had been. Even if Stevie and Lisa had wanted to get a word in edgewise, they wouldn't have been able to. Carole was just too excited.

"The only thing that will be missing on Saturday when I'll be at the racetrack with Judy and Mr. McLeod and"—

she sighed before uttering the name—"Prancer, is that you guys can't be there with me. You've got to meet her, though. She's some horse!"

Stevie winked at Lisa. Carole never even noticed.

CAROLE HAD NEVER seen anything quite like the racetrack. It was an entire world designed for horses. Near the track itself were a few small stalls where the horses were walked and saddled before each race, but that was only for the few horses participating in each race. Beyond that, out of the public's view, was an enormous collection of stables where all of the horses racing at each meet were stabled. The larger racing farms could have as many as sixty horses racing at a meet. The two horses Mr. McLeod had racing that day were housed in temporary stabling next to one another. Prancer and Hold Fast both seemed comfortable in their new quarters.

All around them, in the stable, owners, stable hands, trainers, riders, vets, and assistants to everybody bustled busily, tending to the horses. All of the talk was about horses and money. The owners and trainers each wanted their horse to do well in the races so the horses could win money and become more valuable. Carole was still amazed at this new side of horseback riding, but Judy didn't seem surprised at all. Carole didn't say anything. She just stood in the stable and looked around.

"First time at a track?" a voice asked her. She turned and found herself facing a man about her size. "I'm Stephen," he said, offering his hand. "I'm a jockey and I'm riding for Mr. McLeod."

"Oh, hello," Carole said, taking the young man's hand. She introduced herself and admitted that she never had been to a track before.

"Mr. McLeod told me about the ride you took on Prancer the other day. He said you were really good."

"Me?"

"It was you, wasn't it?" Stephen asked.

Carole blushed. "Yes, it was me," she said. "I just didn't think I'd done such a great job. After all, it was Prancer who did all the work."

"That horse loves to run. Alone. She doesn't seem to have the competitive spirit that really great racers have got to have. I've ridden her on Mr. McLeod's practice track dozens of times. She's fabulous by herself. But when she's pitted up against another horse, I never get that burst of speed from her. Too bad."

"How's that?" Carole asked.

75

Stephen looked at her a little oddly. Then he answered the question. "Well, a racehorse that doesn't race doesn't have much of a future, does she?"

There it was again—business. Dollars and cents. It wasn't enough for a horse to be beautiful, sweet, wonderful, and fast. She had to win, too.

"Couldn't Prancer be used for breeding?" Carole asked.

Stephen shrugged. "Maybe, but it's not for me to say. Still, if a mare isn't fast, doesn't have that spirit, chances are her foals won't either. Anyway, today's race could be telling. We'll see."

"Ah, there you are, Stephen," Mr. McLeod said. "The stallion is going to be in the third race and Prancer in the sixth. There's a mare running in the first race that I'm considering purchasing, so we don't have much time to talk before post time."

Stephen, Mr. McLeod, and the trainer began plotting their strategy for the two races Stephen would ride. They talked quietly, not wanting other owners to overhear. Carole caught some of the words, but much of it didn't mean very much to her. They talked about things like backstretch, quarter pole, and post position. Carole gathered that for Prancer's race, Stephen was to hold back until near the end and then see if he could bring out that burst of speed that had made Prancer such a joy for Carole to ride. The race was going to be a real test of Prancer's abilities.

"We've got this race today, and she's entered in three other races this season," Mr. McLeod said. "If she's got the stuff, we'll see it one of these times. If not, we'll have to see if we can find a home for her someplace else."

Carole felt a nervous twinge. What had Mr. McLeod meant by that? She hoped for Prancer's sake that she won today's race.

Suddenly there was a flurry of activity as a voice over a loudspeaker announced that horses for the first race of the afternoon should be moving to the paddock area next to the track for saddling. A dozen horses were led along the path by their trainers and stable hands. Another group of stable ponies were being saddled quickly and taken along as well by various riders—most much too large to be jockeys—all dressed in breeches and identical shirts.

"Who are they?" Carole asked Judy.

"Those are the lead pony riders. Each horse in a race has a lead pony that goes with it in the post parade. The riders then stand by to help during and after the race in case there's trouble, or if their jockey needs help in the winner's circle. The racehorses all seem to be comforted and calmed by the presence of these ponies. Let's go watch the first race with Mr. McLeod. You'll see."

Together the three of them rode over to the grandstand. As an owner, Mr. McLeod was entitled to watch the race from a box in the clubhouse of the grandstand.

However, as a potential owner, he wanted the opportunity to watch the horse he was considering from track level. They stood by the fence at the edge of the track. A man came out onto the track and blew a long horn. It was the kind of horn Carole had seen at horse shows, only he was blowing the familiar racetrack tune known as "First Call." Immediately thereafter the horses, accompanied by their lead ponies, filed out onto the track. The horses circled around the track, sometimes walking, sometimes going faster, but in each case obviously warming up. On the far side of the track, there was a portable starting gate set up. By the time the horses reached it, the lead ponies pulled back and the horses entered the little compartments that they'd start to race from.

A bell rang, the gates opened, and the race began. Then the whole thing was over in about two minutes.

Carole had completely lost track of where the horse that Mr. McLeod was watching had come in or how it had raced. However, one look at Mr. McLeod told her that the horse had done well. He was nodding sagely to himself.

"She ran a nice race," Judy said, showing that she had noticed many things Carole hadn't. Oh well, Carole thought, I'm just going to have to learn to watch carefully and understand what I'm watching before it makes much sense. At least she had been able to tell which horse had won. Of course, there wasn't any trick to that.

The winning horse's number, as well as those of the sec-
ond-, third-, and fourth-place finishers, were posted on
the large "tote board" in front of her. Besides that, they
were standing right in front of the winner's circle. The
first-place horse was being photographed while his jockey
stood on a scale, holding the saddle and blanket on the
scale with him. That was to make sure how much weight
the horse had been carrying. Other riders took their
horses back to the paddock, accompanied by the lead
ponies and their riders. Already the track was being prepared for the next race, which would take place in a half
an hour.

Carole and Judy returned to the stable area while Mr.
McLeod went to find the owner of the horse he'd been
watching. He was prepared to buy the horse right there
and then. Carole was pretty sure that the next time she
saw him, he'd have a new mare for his stable.

Stephen was nowhere in sight. Judy explained that he
was in the jockey's dressing room, preparing for his first
race. Hold Fast, who was going off in the third race, was
getting a lot of attention from the groom and stable
hand. Although there was no scientific way to explain it,
everybody always agreed that a well-groomed horse ran
faster. Carole's own theory about that was that horses
were quite vain. They knew when they looked good, and
they enjoyed showing it off. She'd never seen anything
about a horse that would disprove that theory. The stal-

lion was clearly enjoying all the attention he was getting. His coat gleamed. So did his eyes. At the groom's suggestion, Carole picked up a brush and helped with the grooming. If the stallion had liked two people working on his coat at once, he would *love* having three people do it!

When it came time to take Hold Fast over to the paddock, the groom handed the lead rope to Carole.

"Why don't you walk him over?" he said. "He's got the third post position, so he'll be in the stall marked with a three."

It was all Carole could do to keep from asking "*Me?!*" when he handed her the rope. Without a word, because she couldn't have talked anyway, she clipped the lead onto the stallion and walked him the quarter mile of soft dirt track to the paddock behind the grandstand. She was walking with a dozen other grooms and caretakers, but she felt more special than all of them, and she felt certain that everybody was looking at her. A glance around, however, told her that nobody was noticing. Everybody was simply doing their job. What a wonderful, exciting job it is, Carole thought.

Once she'd delivered the stallion to the groom in the paddock, Carole watched the stallion and all the other horses go through their final preparations. Each horse was tacked up with the same kind of very small racing saddle, and each horse was given a number, representing its post position. Carole had learned that the post position basically meant which stall the horse started the race in, and how far off the rail the horse would be. Being close to the rail usually gave a horse an advantage, unless it was the kind of horse who wasn't comfortable riding in a pack and needed space. In those cases the owners hoped for a higher post position. Mr. McLeod had seemed happy with the third post position for Hold Fast. That was good enough for Carole.

While the horses were being saddled up, a lot of other activity was going on. At first glance, Carole thought it was just confusion, but by watching and listening, she realized it was not. Each horse was inspected by three different track officials. She asked Stephen what that was about.

"The first man is the paddock judge. He's checking to see that all the equipment on the horse is authorized. Riders and trainers can't change the kind of tack a horse uses without notifying the paddock judge and getting approval. The second man, in this case a woman—the lady with the blue windbreaker—is checking the horses' lip tattoos for identification."

Carole watched while the woman checked the upper lip of each of the horses, compared what she saw with information she carried on a clipboard, and then moved on.

"Every registered racing Thoroughbred has a number tattooed on its lip," Stephen continued. "The identifier's job is to be sure the horse is who the owner says it is. Then the third person is the track veterinarian. He's checking to be sure all the horses are in good health, and he has the right to 'scratch' any horse he's not sure of. He's especially looking for lameness now. He's already drawn blood for a drug test. See, a horse under the influence of medication has an advantage over unmedicated horses."

"That's not fair to the other horses, is it?" Carole asked.

"No," Stephen replied, "but even more important, it's not fair to the people who are betting on the horses. The rule is that no horse can receive *any* medication within two days of a race."

Again Carole was learning about money and horses. This time, though, it wasn't the owner or rider, but the spectator whose money was involved.

When all the judges finished examining the horses, the paddock judge called, "Riders up!" and it was almost time for the race to begin.

Stephen and Hold Fast circled the ring in the paddock one more time for the spectators and then walked sedately along the pathway onto the main track, accompanied by the lead ponies. Carole stationed herself by the finish line as Mr. McLeod and Judy had done at the earlier race. She didn't know where they were right then, but that was all right. If she was going to learn to watch a race, she wanted to watch it by herself. She could ask questions later.

The bell rang. The horses were off. Stephen had said that the stallion was a steady runner and liked being in front of the pack. Just as Carole had expected, Stephen tried to move up to the front as quickly as possible. He spent most of the race in second place, trailing a horse who seemed to be flying. Then, suddenly, the lead horse fell back, apparently tired. Stephen and Hold Fast took over the lead. For a while it looked as if they'd keep it, but a few horses who had been holding back in the pack pulled up toward the front. In the last section of the race—the homestretch, Stephen had called it—two horses pulled in front of the stallion, putting the stallion back into third place.

Carole thought that was too bad. It seemed a little disappointing to come in third, but then she saw Stephen's face as he slowed down and stopped the horse, finally turning him around to return to the paddock. He was clearly thrilled with the outcome. Then Carole remembered. Mr. McLeod had expected the horse to come in fifth. Third place was pretty darn good! She smiled and waved at Stephen. He waved back. A few people standing near her looked at her. They were pretty surprised that she was waving at a jockey.

"He's a friend," she said, very proudly. She was going

to turn and head for the stables once again when she heard a shriek. There was something familiar about the shriek, something almost friendly about it. Carole could have sworn that someone was even shrieking her name, but that wasn't possible, was it?

"Caaaarrrrroooooooollllle!"

She turned and looked up. Someone was definitely shrieking her name, and it was none other than Stevie Lake! And there, standing next to Stevie, was Lisa. The two of them were in the first deck of the grandstand, with Stevie's parents. That was about the last thing Carole had expected.

"Wait there!" Stevie called.

In a matter of seconds Lisa and Stevie were by her side. They were both thrilled about the third-place finish Stephen had gotten on the stallion.

"My father even won some money on him," Stevie said. "Because of that, he's decided the whole idea of coming to the races today was his in the first place!"

The girls laughed. "There's so much to tell you guys," Carole began breathlessly. "You just wouldn't believe everything that goes on here and everything I'm learning. This whole place, this whole thing—horse racing, I mean—is another world. It's hard to believe it's all done with the same animals we love so much at Pine Hollow."

"Purebred Thoroughbreds aren't exactly what we're

riding at Pine Hollow," Lisa reminded her. "Except for Topside, I mean."

"But they're all horses, aren't they?" Stevie reasoned.

"You'd hardly think so, sticking around here," Carole told her. "It's more like they're some kind of precious commodity."

"I don't know about you, but that's just the way *I* feel about horses," Stevie said.

"Me, too, definitely," Carole agreed. "But it's more than that. It's money. It's business. It's something we never think about."

"I think about money all the time," Stevie said.

"That's because you always spend everything you've got," Lisa said drily. "To you, two dollars is a precious commodity. I think what Carole's saying is that these animals are worth hundreds of thousands of dollars, and they're treated as if they're royalty."

"Yes," Carole said. "That's it, exactly. We're used to horses that may be worth a couple of thousand dollars, which isn't exactly pocket change, but these horses are worth zillions. That's a big difference."

"You can say that again," Stevie agreed, finally understanding Carole's point.

"Carole?"

Carole turned. It was Mr. McLeod.

"I'm glad I found you. I need your help. Can you get to the stables quickly?"

"Sure," she said. "I'm coming now." She waved good-bye to Lisa and Stevie and followed the owner, who was walking very quickly. "What's up?" she asked.

"It's Prancer," he said. "She's getting fidgety. You seem to have a way of calming her. Did you bring any riding clothes?"

"I have some in Judy's truck," she said. "I came here straight from my Pony Club meeting this morning."

"Good," he said. "Go change in the ladies' room at the stable. I want you to ride Prancer's lead pony instead of the track's lead rider. I'll have the groom bring you a track shirt so you'll match the others. You're going to have to hurry, though. Post time is in about forty minutes."

Hurry? Mr. McLeod didn't have to worry about that. She was so excited, she was just about flying!

9

TWENTY MINUTES LATER Carole was wearing her own breeches and boots and a shirt with the name of the racetrack on it. She found herself looking down frequently, just to be sure it was true. The other lead riders looked at her oddly, but since Mr. McLeod had said she was going to be Prancer's lead rider, they had to accept her. One of the grooms gave her the reins to a pony, boosted her up into the saddle, and then, just like magic, she was a lead rider.

Her duties had been explained carefully but quickly. She was to hold a lead rope on Prancer to take her to the paddock, just as she'd done with the stallion, only this time she was mounted on her own pony. After Prancer had been tacked up and had walked around the paddock a few times, showing her stuff for the few spectators who had come to see the horses there, the lead riders would proceed under the grandstand to the track where the post parade would begin. She was to use her judgment about what might be necessary to calm Prancer down. She took the lead rope and clicked her tongue. Prancer responded immediately. She didn't seem in the least bit nervous. Perhaps Judy and Mr. McLeod were right, that all Prancer needed was to have Carole around. It was very flattering, of course, but Carole found it hard to believe.

When she arrived at the paddock, the groom told her to dismount and to walk Prancer around the paddock ring twice for the spectators. It turned out that the spectators included a lot of bettors and two very excited Saddle Club members.

"Carole!" Stevie called out.

Carole looked up and grinned, waving at her friends.

"Is it real?" Lisa asked.

"It is," Carole assured them. "Mr. McLeod wanted me to do this because he thinks I have this magical ability to calm this filly down. Isn't it weird? She isn't nervous or upset at all!" Then, as if Prancer were trying to prove Carole right, she walked right up to Lisa and Stevie and began nuzzling them for a treat or a pat.

Stevie and Lisa couldn't believe their good luck.

"She's beautiful!" Lisa said, barely able to utter the words because she was so excited.

88

"And loving!" Stevie added. "I'm sure she's going to win. I'll tell my dad to bet a bundle on her."

"Let your dad do his own betting," Carole advised. "But for now, go back to your seats. I'm going to be in the post parade, and I want to see somebody cheering for Prancer."

"I'll cheer for Prancer, but I'm mostly going to cheer for you," Stevie said. She and Lisa gave Prancer a final good-bye pat and returned to the grandstand.

The next few minutes went very quickly for Carole. She was glad she'd taken the time to understand what was going on at the time of the earlier race, because now it all seemed a blur, made fuzzier by the butterflies in her stomach.

"Riders up!" the judge announced. Carole wasn't certain, but she thought that included her. She remounted her pony, glanced around and saw that all the other lead riders were mounted as well, and then she took Prancer's lead, holding it while Stephen hopped onto the feather-weight saddle Prancer was now sporting.

Carole tried to do everything the other lead riders were doing. As each racehorse reached the entrance to the track, its assigned lead pony took the lead, escorting the horse and jockey out onto the track. It wasn't hard to do that. Prancer seemed to want to be as close as possible to Carole. She walked her pony slowly, savoring every second of the parade. The horses circled back toward the end of the grandstand and then began their trek around the track to the starting gate. The Thoroughbreds were all carefully in line by their numbers, allowing the spectators to see and admire them. They walked slowly and sedately. That wasn't easy for Carole, because she kept craning her neck to see Stevie and Lisa. Once she spotted them, she waved. None of the other lead riders was waving, but then probably none of them had their best friends in the grandstand, she reasoned. She glanced at Stephen to see if she'd made a mistake. He just winked at her and then leaned forward and patted Prancer's neck. Prancer nodded her head eagerly.

The track was bigger than Carole had imagined. It was wider than Mr. McLeod's practice track, and it seemed longer, too, though that may have been because the whole place, including the grandstand, seemed so vast. The crowd milled anxiously—some spectators headed for betting windows, others for hot-dog stands. Children played in open spaces that would soon hold eager race watchers. Some of the people watched every horse's every move. Others studied booklets or newspapers. A few dozed on the benches in the sun. Everybody seemed to be enjoying a day at the track, one way or another.

Carole spotted Mr. McLeod then, standing at the same place along the rail so he could watch the race for himself. Judy stood next to him. She thought of waving to them but decided it would be unprofessional. Then Mr. McLeod waved at her. She waved back.

"Warm-up time," Stephen said. All around them, the racehorses began cantering and galloping toward the starting gate. Carole pulled her pony away to allow Stephen and Prancer the space they needed to stretch Prancer's muscles for the race. Stephen didn't want Prancer to trot or canter. He made her gallop from a standing start, just as she would do in the race. Carole watched Prancer, once again awestruck by the beauty of her movements and the perfection of her speed. She felt she could watch that horse for hours. She was sorry the whole race was going to be over so quickly.

Stephen and Prancer galloped a quarter of the way around the track and then slowed to an elegant and graceful walk the rest of the way to the starting gate. Carole and the other lead riders withdrew to a special area where they were to wait until the end of the race.

"You stay here until that horse is ready to go back to the paddock," one of the other lead riders told Carole, but she already knew that. She just nodded, trying to pretend she was grateful for the tidbit of information. Nobody else seemed to have any other words of wisdom for her. She waited.

Soon she saw that the horses were all being put into the starting gate. It would be only seconds now. Prancer went into her little slot without any complaint. Carole could barely see from where she was, but she thought Prancer's ears were perked up and turning rapidly. That was a good sign. It meant that Prancer was alert to everything that was happening around her. She'd run a good race.

The bell rang.

"And they're off!" the public-address system blasted out. The words that followed were a blur. So much of Carole's attention was centered on what she was watching that she couldn't possibly take in the announcer's words.

Prancer burst out of the gate, immediately taking the lead. But that wasn't what was supposed to happen. Stephen was supposed to hold her back until the last part of the race, when he'd been told to make her go as fast as she could. Carole watched Prancer carefully, and the look of the horse told her that nothing was going to stop her. The horse who loved to run fast by herself, alone on the practice track, wanted the utter joy of running by herself, ahead of the rest of the field on the racetrack. Prancer's legs flew back and forth so fast Carole couldn't even see them land. Stephen had sensed the urgency in the horse's gait and had given her all the rein she needed to run wild and free, ahead of everybody else.

Even from across the track, Carole was sure she could

hear the pounding of Prancer's hoofbeats, so rapid as to be a single throbbing sound.

And then something happened. Prancer stumbled. Her right foreleg bent gruesomely under her body. Stephen's arms flew up in protest, and the reins jerked away. Prancer's other three legs tried to carry the burden, to continue the race, but then all four legs seemed to collapse at once. To Carole's horror Prancer stumbled a final time and fell forward, as awkwardly as she had been graceful just a few seconds before.

Stephen was thrown so completely off balance by the sudden forward and downward pitch of his mount that he flew into the air, off Prancer's right side.

Then, suddenly, Prancer wasn't alone. A crowd of racing horses bore down on her, each rider desperately trying to avoid hitting the downed horse and equally desperately trying to avoid her rider. Stephen rolled away from the path of the oncoming field of racers as fast as he could, just barely escaping the deadly hooves.

The second the other horses had passed the downed Prancer and Stephen, many things happened. An ambulance rolled onto the track, headed for Stephen. The track vet hurried toward Prancer. Judy and Mr. McLeod broke out of the grandstand, running for the horse and rider as well. The crowd called words of encouragement and concern.

Carole saw and heard none of this. All she could see was Prancer, lying in the dirt, crying out in pain. Without knowing what she was doing, Carole kicked her pony to action. The horse sprang at her touch, dashing across the track to where Prancer was lying and unable to move. Images flashed through her mind, images of horses who had to be destroyed because of injuries; images of horses who had died because of carelessness; images of horses who wouldn't live to ride again. She saw death and pain. And she saw Prancer.

Carole was the first person to arrive at the horse's side. Stephen was pulling himself up and seemed okay. Carole dismounted and turned her attention to Prancer. As soon as the horse saw Carole, she stopped crying so loudly. Carole didn't think she was in any less pain, it was just that she seemed to feel comforted by Carole's presence. Her cry turned to a whimper.

Although she didn't want to, Carole automatically reached for the filly's right leg. It was the one that had collapsed under her. It was almost certain that was where the trouble lay, and Carole was terribly afraid of what she would find. A racehorse with a broken leg was useless on the track. No matter how much an owner loved it, he might not be able to keep it. Many severely injured racehorses met the same sad end. Carole didn't even want to think about it.

She didn't feel any breaks in Prancer's leg, though she

wasn't sure she would have known one if she had. She was more sure that if she touched a place where the bone was broken that Prancer would call out again. The horse remained still and quiet. Then Carole's hand felt the hoof. It was hot. She checked Prancer's left front hoof. It was not hot.

"How is she?" Judy asked breathlessly.

"It's in her right hoof," Carole informed her automatically. "Here, feel." She stood up and stepped back to allow room for Judy to examine the horse. The instant Carole was out of Prancer's field of vision, the horse began crying loudly again.

Carole stepped closer and then sat down cross-legged on the track, holding Prancer's head on her lap. She stroked the horse's cheek and neck calmly, talking all the while.

"It's okay, girl," she said. "Judy's here. She'll take care of you. She'll find out what's wrong, and she's going to know what to do to make you better so you can race again and lead the field again and cross the finish line again. And I'll be there with you, cheering and calling your name, and I'll hold your trophies and then I'll hug you in the winner's circle."

"What's the story?" the track vet asked Judy when he arrived.

Judy stood up, and the two of them walked a few steps away to talk about Prancer's condition. Mr. McLeod joined them. The three talked in low voices. Carole couldn't hear what they were saying, but she was afraid she knew.

"Prancer, my beautiful Prancer," she said, hugging the horse, hoping that the love that flowed through her arms would heal the filly and save her life.

"She's a good horse, you know," Stephen said.

"I know," Carole said, lifting her head from Prancer's cheek. She noticed the cheek was moist with her own tears. She hadn't even known she'd been crying.

"I never saw her run like that, you know. Mr. McLeod was right. You were a good omen for her. She was running for you. She was going to win the race or die trying," Stephen said.

Carole glanced at him sharply. "Is that what this is about?" she asked. "Do the horses have to sacrifice themselves to win?"

"No," he said. "But it happens. And when it does, often it's because the horse wanted it that way."

"Prancer wanted to die?"

"No," he said. "She wanted to win."

Carole looked down at the beautiful white-faced bay who rested her head so peacefully on Carole's lap. When the next tear landed on the rich brown fur of the horse's cheek, Prancer blinked, then nodded calmly, as if she were trying to reassure Carole and tell her it was all right.

"Let's see if she can stand now," Mr. McLeod said to Carole. "Want to help her up?"

Carole realized he was speaking to her. Very gently she stood up herself. Then she took Prancer's reins and began to encourge the horse to rise. The act of rising from a lying position could be awkward for even the most agile and healthy horse. Horses had very long and slender legs compared to the heavy weight they were each expected to carry. When one of those legs didn't work properly, the procedure was agonizing—at least it was for Carole.

She helped Prancer balance, encouraging her to put weight on her left foreleg, rather than on the damaged right. There was not a sound from the spectators. They all knew, just as Carole did, that the next few seconds were going to be critical to Prancer's life. If she couldn't even stand, they might decide to put her out of her pain right then and there. Carole didn't want that to happen. She couldn't let that happen. No way!

"Come on, girl," Carole said. "First this one. That's the way."

She talked, she coaxed, she soothed. She even sang. It didn't seem odd to her that she was surrounded by adults, all horse professionals, each of whom had many times the experience with horses that she did, and each of whom was waiting for her, Carole Hanson, to perform the miracle they hoped for.

Prancer shifted her weight and brought her hind legs directly under her. That was what she had to do first. Now she had to get the left foreleg where it could carry the necessary weight.

"I don't know about this. . . ." the track vet began.

Mr. McLeod shushed him. "This horse loves this girl. That can be a powerful medicine," he said.

Carole concentrated on what she was doing and how Prancer was doing. Prancer's hind legs lifted her flanks. Then she stretched her left foreleg and braced it against the soft earth of the track. Slowly, awkwardly, the horse rose and was, at the end, standing on her three good legs.

The grandstand erupted in a wild ovation.

"They're all cheering for Prancer!" Carole said elatedly.

"No, Carole," Judy corrected her. "They're cheering for you."

Carole looked up at the people who waved and clapped for her. She saw Lisa and Stevie there, too, standing by the rail, crying just as she had been, but smiling and waving in spite of their tears. Mr. and Mrs. Lake beamed proudly and waved as well.

"Let's get Prancer back to the stable," Carole said. "I don't want her to be frightened by all this noise."

"I think she likes it," Mr. McLeod said. "Look at her."

Carole turned and took a look at the horse she was leading so slowly. Prancer whimpered with pain at every step she took, but her ears were perked straight up and twitching alertly. This was a horse who was driven by success, by winning, by the roar of a crowd. This was a horse who wanted to live. But, Carole wondered, what did she have to live for?

ONCE PRANCER WAS back in the stable, Judy took charge, calling for the portable X-ray machine. Dozens of people hovered, watching and asking questions. Stewards and judges watched every move that Judy made. The track veterinarian assisted Judy. Nobody needed Carole anymore.

She drew back from the crowd. She was frightened when she realized that most of the people were there to see if it would be necessary to put Prancer to sleep. Mr. McLeod watched silently. Carole could tell from the look on his face that the same thing was on his mind. He excused himself for a moment then, saying something about having to call his insurance company.

Carole fled. She couldn't take any more. She loved horses so much, and she thought Prancer was such a wonderful horse, that she couldn't bear the idea that Prancer might not make it—that that very special horse might have to be traded for mere insurance money.

There were three more races to run at the track. Beyond the confines of Mr. McLeod's stalls in the stabling area, racetrack life seemed to be going on in very much the same way that it had been before. The lead riders rode their ponies with the racehorses. Trainers delivered last-minute words of advice to jockeys. Spectators studied horses, studied programs, studied the lines in their hands, and the formation of clouds, hoping to find a good way to pick a winning horse to bet on.

But for Carole everything had changed. All she wanted to do was get away from the track and be alone. Finally she found a place where nobody else was. It was the feed-storage shed for the stables. She opened a door and entered, finding herself in a vast room stacked with bales of hay and barrels of grain. The sweet and familiar smell of the hay welcomed her. She sat on one bale, plucked a piece of hay from another, and chewed on it.

So much had happened in the last couple of weeks. First she'd had to deal with Starlight's injury and Pepper's growing old. While working with Judy she'd also found out about lots of other illnesses and injuries that horses could get. And then she'd discovered for some people horses were mainly a business, one that would continue even though a beautiful racehorse had just been seriously injured. What will come next? Carole wondered. When will I have learned enough of the lessons of life and death? Right now it seemed as if she were being forced to learn them again and again.

The tears came then, trickling at first and then streaming. She cried for Prancer, for her owner and rider and how much they loved the little filly. She cried for Cobalt, another horse she'd loved who had had to be destroyed. She even cried for her mother, now gone over two years, but still a painfully wonderful memory. She cried because she felt sadness and grief. She cried because she was afraid.

The shed door cracked open, letting in a stream of light that fell across the bales of hay.

"Carole?"

She looked up. Stevie and Lisa had found her. Without a word her two best friends ran to her and hugged her. They understood. They understood everything, and they were there to help her—or were they there to give her bad news?

"Prancer?" Carole asked, uttering the whole question with a single word.

"Judy's reading the X ray now."

"I can't stand it," Carole said.

"We know," Stevie said, hugging Carole some more. "But I think Prancer needs you."

That was the one thought that could get Carole back on her feet. If Prancer needed her, she'd be there for her.

"We saw her and she seemed glad to see us," Lisa explained. "Except she kept looking over my shoulder."

"I think she was looking for you," Stevie said.

"She's an amazing horse," Carole said, smiling for the first time in a while. It made her smile to remember how much Prancer seemed to like her and her friends. Horses didn't usually become attached to one person or another, but Prancer had become attached to Carole immediately. She recalled the first time she'd seen the filly in her stall at Maskee Farms, when she'd reached right over to Carole and nuzzled her. "A truly amazing horse," Carole repeated.

"All the more reason to be there for her now," Stevie said, offering Carole a hand.

Carole took it. She also took the tissue that Lisa offered her. The three girls left the feed shed and returned to the stables together.

Carole was very frightened as they approached Prancer's stall. The filly was still completely surrounded by official-looking people jotting notes on clipboards and talking into recording devices. At the center of it all were Judy, the track veterinarian, and Mr. McLeod. They were holding a large X ray up to the light to study it. Carole didn't want to know what they were saying. She just wanted to be with Prancer. She walked past Judy, straight to the horse. Lisa and Stevie followed.

Prancer stood uneasily on three legs, her right foreleg lifted awkwardly from the floor of the stall. Carole reached into her pocket and pulled out a sugar lump, which she gave to the horse. It was comforting to hear the familiar crunch of the horse's teeth as she nibbled at the irresistible sweet. Carole didn't usually give horses treats, but Prancer seemed to be so deserving and, after all, what difference did it make if she got a little spoiled now?

Carole gave her a big hug. Prancer nuzzled her back affectionately. Lisa patted the filly's neck. Stevie picked up a grooming brush and began tending to her. Each girl knew that these things might not matter at all, but it seemed that the only thing they could do for the horse was to treat her normally. In spite of the considerable pain in her foot, Prancer nodded her head approvingly. Just like any other horse, this precious racer was vain and loved attention. If that was what she loved, The Saddle Club was determined to give it to her.

"Too bad," the track veterinarian said.

In spite of herself, Carole listened.

"Not really," Mr. McLeod said. "The insurance money would be nice, and I know I'll never recover my investment, but look at that horse. Would anybody want to destroy her?"

At his words everybody standing around the stall

looked at Prancer, preening proudly under the affectionate attention of three adoring girls.

Judy looked in surprise and then burst into laughter. Carole and her friends realized how foolish they must have looked, tending to the grooming of a horse whose life was on the line. Carole released her hug. Stevie took the grooming brush in her other hand.

"What's the story?" Stevie asked Judy. Carole was glad she'd asked. No matter how badly she wanted to know, she knew she couldn't have done it herself.

"Prancer has a broken bone in her foot," Judy began. She held up the X ray to show, but it was hard to see. "It's her pedal bone, and the fracture extends to the coffin joint. She's never going to race again."

"Oh, no," Carole said involuntarily. "What does . . ."

"It means she can't race. It doesn't mean she can't live. The bone will heal with proper care, but she'll always tend to favor it, and if she races again and favors her right foot, she'll run a great risk of breaking something more serious."

"Will she become a brood mare?" Carole asked. She could see Prancer spending the rest of her days becoming the mother of championship racing horses.

"Mr. McLeod?" Judy asked, turning the question to him.

"I don't think so," he said. "The fact is that Prancer's father also broke his pedal bone, and now that she's had an accident in the same bone, I suspect it's a hereditary fault. That's not a good characteristic to pass on to a foal, and certainly not one who is meant for a racehorse."

"Then, what?" Carole asked.

"I'm not sure yet," he said. "I'll just have to see what I can do. In a way it would be easier to take the insurance money, but Prancer's a gem of a horse, with the sweetest disposition I've ever had in my stable. She should be with people, I think. For now, though, she's going back to Maskee Farms." He paused and looked around. His groom was standing nearby. Mr. McLeod told him to load up Hold Fast and the mare he'd bought after the first race. Then he turned to Carole. "You'll be the right one to load Prancer onto the van. Will you do it?"

"I'd be proud to," Carole said.

Once the other two horses were in their compartments, Carole clipped a lead rope onto Prancer's halter and began urging the horse toward the van. Lisa and Stevie were with her every step of the way, patting and talking to Prancer.

"Come on, girl," Carole said. "Just a little walk and then a nice ride. Nobody's going to let anything bad happen to you." There was a catch in Carole's throat as she said the words. She thought about the spectacular race that Prancer had been running, and it made her very sad to know that the horse would never cross the finish line again. Still, she was going to live, and for now that was enough.

Slowly Prancer made her way to the van, hobbling awkwardly in pain. She never complained, though, because she was comforted by the presence of Carole and her friends. Carole didn't know if Prancer would be able to make it up the steep incline of the ramp that led into the van. She asked one of the grooms to bring another ramp, longer and more level. It would be easier for Prancer. The filly seemed grateful as she looked at the gentle incline ahead into the van. Carole didn't pause. She knew if she hesitated, Prancer would sense her concern. Carole tugged softly on the lead rope, and Prancer began the climb on her three good legs as if she'd been doing it that way all of her life. Once the filly was in the van, Carole secured the lead rope and then turned around to look at Prancer. Then she put her arms around the filly's neck and gave her a big hug.

"You okay in there?" Judy asked.

"I'm fine," Carole assured her. "Can I ride back to the stable with the horses?"

"Not in the van," Judy said. "Even the most wonderful horse can get fussy on a ride when she's injured. The groom will be with Prancer. It's just not safe for you. Come on out of there. Besides, Stevie and Lisa have come up with an interesting idea, and I think I need your help."

What did that mean? Carole wondered. She slipped out under the lead rope and hopped down out of the van. Lisa and Stevie were standing next to Judy. Stevie had a grin on her face that told Carole something was definitely up.

"Have you had one of your wild and crazy ideas?" Carole asked.

"Not me," Stevie said. "It's all Lisa's idea. See, we two are switching roles these days. I'm the one who's helping her with her homework, and she's the one coming up with schemes."

"Is the world turning upside down?" Carole asked.

"I *hope* so," Lisa said, grinning mischievously.

"Now that that's settled, will somebody tell me where the nearest phone is?" Judy asked.

"Right over there," Lisa and Stevie said at once, pointing. Obviously they'd done some homework on the scheme, too.

Judy headed for the phone.

"What's going on?" Carole asked.

"Just you wait and see," Lisa said.

"Yeah, just wait."

Carole didn't seem to have a choice.

11

CAROLE HAD BEEN so busy with Judy and the racehorses for two weeks that she'd almost forgotten about the big event at Pine Hollow the day after the race—Dorothy DeSoto's demonstration. The "almost" was because of Lisa and Stevie, who had talked about it a lot.

Dorothy was a very special friend to the three girls. They had been staying at her house in New York City when she'd had her accident at the American Horse Show—the accident that had cost her a career as a competitive rider. Since that day she'd spent most of her time at her stable on Long Island breeding and training horses. Her visit to Pine Hollow for a demonstration ride was a very special treat, and true to his word, Max had gotten a big crowd to watch it.

"Hey, look, here she comes!" Stevie said excitedly.

The three girls had gotten to Pine Hollow early to tend to Starlight, whose leg was now really improving, and to get front-row seats. Since the demonstration was scheduled to begin at one o'clock, Lisa said she thought it was a bit excessive that they'd gotten there at eight in the morning. Stevie and Carole didn't agree. There was no way they weren't going to have the best seats in the house!

The girls waved cheerfully at Dorothy, who waved back. Then, leaving their programs across their seats to reserve them, they ran over to greet her.

"I groomed Topside especially well for you," Stevie said.

"He looks wonderful!" Dorothy said. "I can see you're taking good care of him all the time, not just for my visit. Thank you."

"Thank me? Thank you for selling him to Max. He's just the greatest! I told him you were coming, too."

Dorothy smiled at Stevie. "I thought so. He didn't seem the least bit surprised to see me," she teased.

Max cleared his throat. "This helloing and joking is all very fine and good," he said. "But according to my watch, there are only fifteen minutes until Dorothy's demonstration is scheduled to begin, and I know she's going to want to do some more warm-ups with Topside. Why don't you all return to your front-row seats? Oh, and Stevie . . ."

"Yes, Max?"

"Are you all ready with—"

"Yes, Max," she said, cutting him off. "I'm all ready."

Max and Dorothy walked together to the stable.

"What's that about?" Carole asked, aware that something was up.

Stevie got a look on her face. It was a look that Carole and Lisa knew well. It meant she had a secret that she was just dying to share but had to keep to herself for now.

"Think we can talk her out of it?" Lisa asked Carole.

"No way," Stevie said. "Just wait, though. Just wait."

Carole shrugged. There seemed to be quite a few secrets in the air these days. At the racetrack yesterday, Judy had reappeared from the telephone booth with a mysterious look on her face and wouldn't say a word about whom she had called or why. Now, today, there was Stevie with her mouth shut tighter than a clam. The positive side of it all was that nobody was looking glum. That made Carole hopeful that none of the secrets were bad ones.

"Ladies and gentlemen, boys and girls," Max began his announcement fifteen minutes later. He was standing in the middle of the ring, and there, waiting to enter, were Topside and Dorothy. Topside's coat was gleaming and perfectly groomed. Stevie had spent a good deal of the morning braiding his mane and tail. He looked just like the championship show horse he was. And in the saddle was a perfectly dressed and balanced Dorothy DeSoto. This was going to be really good.

Dressage was a very difficult type of horseback riding, calling for a near-perfect coordination between the rider and the horse. Stevie knew she was good at it but didn't think she would ever be as expert as Dorothy, though she was willing to try. She planned to watch the demonstration with an eagle eye.

Dorothy DeSoto was quite amazing. Topside, a fine horse every day, was a brilliant horse with Dorothy in the saddle. He responded instantly to every signal Dorothy gave him, and to a lot of signals nobody in the audience could see. Dorothy had chosen to do her demonstration to music, and the audience would have sworn the two of them had been dancing together for years.

At each turn the entire horse's body seemed to curve and then straighten out, one vertebra at a time. At each change of gait, the response was instant and flawless. Every time Topside changed direction and lead, there was no hint of awkwardness. He simply did what was asked of him, and he did it right.

Stevie gripped the fence in front of her, she was so thrilled by what she was watching. Then Dorothy began some of the showy motions of dressage riding. She made Topside appear to be doing a sort of hesitation step and then a skipping step. She also made him walk diagonally to the right and then the left. Stevie and her friends could barely contain themselves. They clapped for both horse and rider as the demonstration continued.

Finally, Dorothy had Topside perform a set of very intricate turns on the forehand, and then he described a series of intertwining circles that filled the entire ring. In the end she had him canter through several figure eights, doing flying lead changes. The audience stood up, clapping by the time she brought Topside to a perfectly balanced halt in the center of the ring. Nobody was clapping louder than The Saddle Club.

"Oh, isn't she wonderful!" Carole uttered.

"She sure is," Lisa agreed.

"She really gives me something to work for," Stevie said.

"You'll do it," Carole said. "I just know you will."

"Well, it helps to have Topside right here, doesn't it?" Stevie asked. "Then I know for sure he knows how to do all that stuff, so if I forget, he can remember for me!"

"It doesn't work that way," Carole said.

"I know," Stevie said. "I was just hoping. . . ."

Dorothy took her final bow and rode out of the ring. Even at a walk she was a wonderful rider. The girls couldn't keep their eyes off her and almost didn't notice when Max reappeared in the ring.

People were beginning to stand up to go, but Max signaled them to sit down.

"We're not quite done yet this afternoon," he began. "We have another treat in store for you, and it's something that will mean a great deal to a lot of the people here and really everybody who has ever ridden at Pine Hollow." He turned to Stevie. "Ready?" he asked. Stevie nodded and left her seat, leaving Lisa and Carole to wonder what on earth was going on.

"About twenty years ago my father bought a new horse for this stable," Max said. "He was an unpromising gray that had had five previous owners. Nobody thought he was much of a horse because he was so gentle. He'd failed as a competition horse, he'd failed as a hunter, he'd failed as a farm horse, and he'd failed as a pony for a little girl who lived on a farm nearby. Dad went to visit this horse, and as he usually could, he saw something special there. This horse wasn't sleek enough or strong enough to compete successfully. This horse didn't like the loud distractions of a fox hunt. He wasn't anywhere near strong enough to pull a plow, and, frankly, one little girl just wasn't enough for him. Dad bought the horse whose name had been Clyde and renamed him . . ."

"Pepper," Carole whispered, finishing the sentence for Max. She was beginning to get an idea of what was about to happen, and she liked it a lot.

"Dad's instincts turned out to be one hundred percent

correct," Max continued. "Pepper has been one of the most loved horses at Pine Hollow. He has always been gentle enough for the newest rider, and he's always been spirited enough for the most experienced rider. He's been just about perfect for us. But time has passed and Pepper has aged. He's no longer the strong young gelding Dad bought. He's not even the eager mature horse so many of us have loved. He's old. Actually, in horse years he's even older than I am—he's approaching ninety. At ninety even horses begin having dreams of retirement. We talked about a condominium in Florida for him. We also thought about a nice cruise around the world. When we asked Pepper about these things, all he did was look at the pasture out behind the stable at Pine Hollow. So, in thanks to him for all he's done for us—that is, me and you—we're giving Pepper that pasture. But before we do that, we're going to give him a little send-off, master-minded by one of our own young riders, Ms. Stevie Lake. Stevie?"

All eyes turned to the door to the stable. There was Stevie, mounted on Pepper bareback.

"What's that in her hand?" Lisa asked.

Carole squinted. "Unless my eyes deceive me, it's an oversized cardboard, uh, gold watch!"

Lisa began laughing. So did all the other people in the audience when they saw what Stevie had for Pepper.

"No retirement party is complete without a gold watch," Max remarked.

"And no retirement party is complete without a sentimental farewell," Stevie added.

"Ah, yes," Max said. "Most of the people here in the audience today have ridden at Pine Hollow at one time or another, right?" Heads nodded agreement. "How many of you have ever ridden Pepper?"

A few people hesitated, but soon hands started going up throughout the audience. It was completely amazing, but it seemed that more than two-thirds of the people there had been on Pepper at least once. And it wasn't just the children—it was their parents as well.

"Look, there's Ms. Ingleby," Lisa said, waving to her English teacher. Ms. Ingleby didn't notice Lisa's hand waving in the crowd, but Lisa didn't care. She was just pleased that so many people knew and loved Pepper.

"Okay, then, let's give him a real send-off," Max said. "Stevie, you do the honors."

Stevie was a real organizer. She got everybody who had ever ridden Pepper to line up, by age, with the youngest first, to hug the horse good-bye.

The first twenty or so riders were so little that Max had to lift them up so they could hug Pepper. Pepper didn't mind at all. He also didn't mind it when the older kids hugged him. And it didn't seem to bother him when dozens of cameras came out of pockets and purses to record the farewell hugs.

Lisa stood behind Carole, waiting her turn. She felt a little silly because it was a slightly silly thing to be doing, but she also felt that it was the perfect way to say good-bye to Pepper. What she found, listening to the young—and not so young—riders around her, was that Pepper's retirement was a loss she shared with a lot of people. Pepper wasn't Max's horse, or her horse, but in a more real sense, he had been everybody's horse. There was a long line of his riders standing in front of and behind Lisa to prove that. Pepper was a special horse whose life had touched many people's lives, perhaps in ways as special as the way it touched hers.

Then, looking around her, Lisa understood what had been missing from her essay about Pepper. She had only viewed the facts of Pepper's old age and her own sadness at his advancing years. She hadn't understood that life—in this case, Pepper's life—was more than the sum of its parts.

She wanted to go back home right then, fish the essay off of her desk, and finish it. She knew just what she would say.

Pepper's life began in a barn in Willow Creek, Virginia. It will end in a pasture not far from that barn.

That seems like a small accomplishment to some people, but Pepper's contribution to many who have known and loved him cannot be measured by the yards he traveled from birth to death. They have to be measured by the lives he touched.

So now it's time for Pepper to take the final few steps of his journey and head for the pasture behind Pine Hollow. While I feel sad about the end of his days at the stable, I also feel a certain happiness. Pepper has earned the right to his rest because he hasn't just taught me and others about riding, or about aging, or about death. He's also taught us what's important about life. It doesn't matter how far you go. It matters what you do for others along the way.

Lisa smiled to herself. That was better. She decided she would write it up tonight and hand it in to Ms. Ingleby in the morning. It wouldn't change her grade. She'd still get an A. Now, however, she would deserve it.

"Next!" Stevie called out, bringing Lisa back from her thoughts about her essay.

"Oh, Pepper!" one girl cried out lovingly as she grasped the horse's neck for her hug. Lisa was pleased to see that it was Eleanora, the girl from her class who had cried when Ms. Ingleby had read Lisa's essay. Even if Eleanora couldn't ride horses often, it was good to know that the riding she'd done had meant so much to her.

When it was Lisa's turn, it was all she could do to keep from crying as well, but the joy she felt at the rightness of this sentimental farewell kept the tears from her eyes.

"I'll come visit you in the pasture," she promised. "I'll even bring you some carrots, too," she whispered.

She could have sworn Pepper winked at her.

Lisa stepped away from Pepper, allowing the next rider her farewell. She looked at the line behind her. There, standing patiently, were many more children and then the adults, including Max, Ms. Ingleby, and at the very end of the line, Mrs. Reg.

Carole waited for Lisa to join her at the edge of the ring. Like Lisa, she was enjoying watching all the farewells. She was finding, as she often had before, that horses had a lot to teach riders about the way the world worked. Since she'd been working with Judy, she'd seen joy, sadness, and tragedy. Sometimes it was hard to feel so many different emotions all at once. Saying a sweet farewell to Pepper made it seem right, though.

For her part, Stevie was just thrilled with Pepper's send-off. She stood, holding Pepper's lead rope, watching each and every hug and farewell. She couldn't think of a better way to say thank you to the wonderful horse at her side.

After Mrs. Reg gave the last hug, Max announced that there was going to be a small reception in Pepper's new home.

"It's just a little party," Max said. "But we do have refreshments. Stevie tells me that Pepper insisted on selecting the menu, so go help yourselves to some carrot sticks, oatmeal cookies, sugar lumps, and apple juice!"

Carole laughed. That was *just* like Stevie!

12

"HEY, STEVIE, YOU are some kind of genius," Carole said, hugging her friend around the shoulders.

"You really know how to throw a retirement party!" Lisa said.

"Well, it was your idea," Stevie said modestly.

"I never said anything about carrots and oatmeal cookies!"

"Let's put it this way: You inspired me to think it all up when you were talking about the essay you wrote."

"Remind me to inspire you more often," Lisa said, reaching for another oatmeal cookie.

"Hey, this is great!" Dorothy DeSoto said, joining The Saddle Club in Pepper's new pasture. "Stevie, I always knew you were a genius at something, I just wasn't sure what."

Stevie laughed. "I hope this isn't all I'm a genius at," she said. "I suspect there's a limited call for retirement parties for horses."

"You've got that right," Carole agreed. "Not many horses deserve the kind of send-off Pepper is getting. And speaking of that, you two never told me how Lisa liked riding Comanche the other day. How was it?"

Lisa shrugged. "Okay, I guess, but he's not Pepper."

"Few horses are," Dorothy said. "You know, Pepper was the first horse I ever rode."

"You?" Lisa asked.

"Me, too," Stevie said. "Maybe that means one day I'll be as good as you."

"It could be," Dorothy told her. "You're making an awfully good start. Now, tell me what you've all been up to—aside from planning this party."

Suddenly it seemed as if there were hundreds of things the girls wanted to tell Dorothy, including their last adventures with Skye Ransom, whom she'd met in New York, and the fact that Carole had gotten a horse who was now injured. "But getting better every day," Carole added optimistically. Carole told Dorothy about the work she'd been doing with Judy and her very interesting and exciting day at the racetrack the day before. She also told her about Prancer.

"Judy thinks she'll get better, but she's never going to race again," Carole said.

"It's always fascinating to me how unique every individual horse is," Dorothy remarked when Carole told her the story. "This Prancer sounds like a wonderful horse. It's a shame her racing career is over, but I know what a serious injury can mean."

Carole blushed uncomfortably. She hadn't meant to remind Dorothy of the injury that was keeping her from competition.

"Don't worry," she said, sensing Carole's embarrassment. "It's a fact of my life, and the important part is that I've still got a career with horses. It's just a different one. I love breeding and training. Sure, I miss riding, but every once in a while I can have a terrific day like this and have a chance to ride my favorite horse with little risk to my health. When I stop to think about it, I'm pretty lucky. Besides, if I hadn't come here, I never would have known about this retirement party."

"Hey, Judy's here," Stevie said, spotting the blue pickup that had pulled into the driveway. "Are you supposed to be making calls with her today?" she asked Carole.

Carole thought about it for a minute. She didn't think so. Judy had been pretty specific about meeting her Monday afternoon at Starlight's stall to check on his progress. She hadn't said anything at all about Sunday.

"No, I don't know why she's here."

Judy stepped down out of her truck and scanned the crowd. She spotted Carole and kept on looking. Then she walked briskly over to Max and took him aside for a private conversation. As the two of them talked, they each looked up at Carole, then their eyes went back to one another. Max nodded, then shook his head.

Lisa, Stevie, and Dorothy continued chatting about horses and riding, but Carole heard none of it. All of her concentration was on Judy and Max. What were they talking about? Why was she here on a Sunday?

Then Carole thought about Prancer, and she was flooded with dread. Something had happened and it couldn't be good. Carole's mind raced. She became convinced that Judy didn't want her to hear bad news from her and was trying to figure out with Max just how to break it to her. She could take it. She'd had enough bad news in her life to know that she could take it. But Prancer? The beautiful white-faced filly?

"Uh, Carole, could you come over here for a minute?" Max asked.

That made it certain. Good news was delivered in public. Bad news always came in private. She could barely move one foot in front of the other, but she had to know, so she went.

"Uh, Carole, it's about Prancer," Judy began.

"Bad news?" Carole asked.

Judy looked at her puzzled. "No, I don't think so," she said. "I just want to ask you something because I need your help."

Carole glanced at Max. He had a grin on his face from ear to ear. She looked back at Judy.

"What about Prancer?"

"Well, I've been doing a lot of thinking and talking over the last twenty-four hours. First I had to talk to my husband, of course, and then my bank, and then Max. I had this sort of crazy idea, inspired by none other than Stevie."

"Stevie has that effect on people sometimes," Carole said, beginning to get the idea that she was going to like this.

"Prancer can't race again, as we know, and her family history of weak hooves makes it unlikely that she'll be a good racing breeder, though I'm willing to try that. However, what it's absolutely clear that she's totally terrific at is being with young people. I have rarely seen a horse respond so quickly to somebody as she did to you. I also saw the way she wanted to nuzzle with Lisa and Stevie at the track yesterday. With kids she's a dream horse. So, anyway, I decided I would try to talk Max into buying Prancer from Mr. McLeod. He and I are now fifty-fifty owners of the filly. The bad news is that she's going to be laid up with her broken bone for several months, maybe as much as a year, and there's a possibility she'll never heal properly.

"There is, however, an excellent possibility that she may one day be as fine a stable horse for Pine Hollow as, say, Pepper has been for more than twenty years."

Prancer at Pine Hollow? Carole shook her head, hoping her ears would clear up so she could hear all of these things right.

"Here?" she asked when she thought she'd cleared her auditory canals.

"Yes, here," Max said. "Pay attention, Carole." He was trying to sound annoyed, but he wasn't succeeding. He was still grinning, and that made annoyance improbable at best.

"Aye-aye, sir," Carole said, saluting. "But, so what's my part in this?"

"Ah, yes, the hard part," Judy said. Now she was grinning, too. "My deal with Max includes free veterinary services for the horse during her recovery from the broken bone, and I'll certainly stop by frequently to be sure that she's healing well *and* to see that Max's end of our partnership—the boarding arrangement—is being held up as well." She winked at Max. "However, Prancer is going to need to be checked almost daily throughout her convalescence. Since you are here almost every day taking care of Starlight, grooming and exercising him, we were wondering if you would be willing to do a daily check on Prancer as well. See, the problem is that she likes you best. She'll fuss if Max sends somebody like Red into the stable, but for you and your friends, Prancer is just a doll."

Carole could barely bring herself to nod agreement. It

all seemed so unreal. A mere day before she had been sure Prancer was doomed, then she'd become convinced that she'd never see the filly again. Now it was turning out that not only would she see her, but she'd be taking care of her, and one day she and her friends would be able to ride her!

As soon as Judy had Carole's agreement, she began talking about the medical side of Prancer's injury. She was going to have to have a special shoe constructed, and she'd be in her stall at complete rest for at least seven months. Her training could resume when she was totally healed, but it would be a long, slow process. A racehorse was trained for speed, not for pleasure riding. Would Carole be willing to help take care of her and retrain her as well? Yes, she would, Carole told Judy and Max. Definitely.

Carole listened to everything that was said, but as she listened, thoughts of Lisa's essay drifted quickly into her mind. Life. It had cycles and turns. It also seemed to have twists. Some of those were good, some bad. Right then she was in the middle of a good twist. That made her happy.

Eventually Judy and Max finished. Prancer was to be delivered to Pine Hollow the next afternoon. Carole promised to be there right after school.

"Anything else?" Max asked.

There was something Carole needed to do, and she

told Max as much. "I was wondering when that would come up," he said. "Go ahead."

Carole left them then and ran, as fast as she knew how, to where Lisa and Stevie were standing, each munching on a sugar lump and drinking apple juice.

"Have I got news for you!" Carole said.

13

LATER THAT DAY things were quiet at Pine Hollow. All the spectators had gone. Max and Mrs. Reg were taking Dorothy out to dinner. Red had the evening off. The only people there were The Saddle Club, and they were having a meeting in the most logical place they could think of—Pepper's stall.

"Hand me the pitchfork, will you?" Stevie asked Lisa. Not only were they having a meeting, but they were also mucking out the stall. It had been Pepper's home for more than twenty years. As of the next day, it would become Prancer's.

"I don't understand why Pepper can't use this anymore," Lisa said.

"Pepper's going to be outdoors most of the time," Carole explained. "When the weather's bad or when he needs to be indoors for any reason, he can use whatever stall is temporarily free. This stall is in the middle of where most of the permanent horses have their stalls. The stable's newest permanent horse should have it."

"And it's going to be sparkling clean for her," Stevie promised, lifting another forkful of soiled bedding and tossing it into a wheelbarrow.

It was a tradition at Pine Hollow that each horse had an assigned stall and that its name appeared on a plaque outside of it. There wasn't time to get a new plaque made for Prancer before she arrived, but Lisa, who was very artistic, had been assigned the job of making a temporary one from the paper and pens on Mrs. Reg's desk. She was having fun doing decorative lettering. She even managed to draw a picture of the reindeer she thought Prancer had been named after.

"Hey, cool," Carole said. "Prancer's going to love that!"

"You mean she's so fantastic she can even read?" Stevie teased.

Carole laughed at herself. "I guess not," she said. "But let me put it this way—*I'm* going to love it."

"That's better," Stevie said, hauling the last of the old bedding out of the stall.

The girls then hosed the stall down and brushed it vigorously, making the floor as clean as possible. They wanted to wait until it dried before covering it with fresh straw. That would take a few minutes. Never one to allow a chance to talk to pass, Stevie turned over a few water buckets and invited her friends to sit with her in the stall.

"Now all we need is ice cream sundaes," Lisa suggested brightly.

Carole laughed.

"Another one of your schemes!" Stevie said.

"Are you jealous because your scheming is contagious?" Carole asked.

"A little, I suppose," Stevie admitted. "Though if it's true that imitation is the sincerest form of flattery, then I guess I'm flattered."

"Just what I had in mind," Lisa said.

One of the things that all of the girls liked about their friendship was that there was no competition among them. They simply enjoyed being together and doing things together—especially horseback riding.

"This has been an odd time," Lisa remarked. "I mean for more reasons than because I'm scheming and Stevie has been helping me with my homework."

"Yes, a lot of weird stuff has been going on," Stevie said, confirming Lisa's feelings. "A lot of things that seemed like bad news have sort of turned out to be good news."

"Even Starlight's injury," Carole said. "If it hadn't been for that, I never would have been with Judy, and I never would have gotten to the racetrack."

"And been the star of the sixth race," Lisa said. "Nobody noticed who won that race. They just noticed what you did with the injured horse."

"And the injury that seemed so bad that turned out to be such good news for us," Stevie said. "See what I mean about things being turned upside down and all for the good?"

"Not all," Carole said. "What about the horse that died of tetanus?"

"And what about the foal that you met?" Lisa said, reminding her of the good side of that day.

"And then there's Pepper's retirement that seemed sad, but that Stevie managed to make into a lot of fun."

"And if it hadn't been for that, Max probably wouldn't have agreed to buy Prancer with Judy."

"Things change," Carole said.

"That's like what I think I was trying to say in my essay about life," Lisa agreed.

"Sometimes it's sad, sometimes it's happy. Old horses move on, new ones are born, some are injured, others heal," Carole continued. "But nothing is ever the same."

"Well, something is," Stevie said. Her friends both looked at her. "The Saddle Club," she said. "It's always wonderful."

There was no arguing that.

ABOUT THE AUTHOR

BONNIE BRYANT is the author of more than fifty books for young readers, including novelizations of movie hits such as *Teenage Mutant Ninja Turtles* and *Honey, I Shrunk the Kids,* written under her married name, B. B. Hiller.

Ms. Bryant began writing The Saddle Club in 1986. Although she had done some riding before that, she intensified her studies then and found herself learning right along with her characters Stevie, Carole, and Lisa. She claims that they are all much better riders than she is.

Ms. Bryant was born and raised in New York City. She lives in Greenwich Village with her two sons.

Taffy Sinclair is perfectly gorgeous and totally stuck-up. Ask her rival Jana Morgan or anyone else in the sixth grade of Mark Twain Elementary. Once you meet Taffy, life will **never** be the same.

Don't Miss Any of the Terrific Taffy Sinclair Titles from Betsy Haynes!

Follow the adventures of Jana and the rest of her friends in **THE FABULOUS FIVE** by Betsy Haynes.